Born in Geraldton, Western Australia, Amanda moved to Perth, Western Australia, to study film & television and creative writing at Murdoch University, earning a BA in Communication Studies. Perth has been her home ever since, aside from a nineteen-month stint in London, England, where she dabbled in Film & TV 'Extra' work.

Amanda is a Scribe Award winner, a two-time Tin Duck Award winner, an Aurealis and Ditmar Award finalist, who primarily writes in the science fiction and thriller genres.

Her works include the sci-fi crime thriller, *The Subjugate*, which is being developed for TV by Anonymous Content and Aquarius Films. *The Subjugate* is also being studied at two German universities (Düsseldorf and Cologne) as part of a program on Australian speculative fiction, in conjunction with the Centre for Australian Studies.

Amanda wrote the Scribe Award winning procedural thriller, *Pandemic: Patient Zero*, which was the first novel set in the *Pandemic* board game universe.

She's also written for Marvel in their X-Men universe, as well as for Black Library in their Warhammer 40k universe.

To keep up to date with new releases visit:
amandabridgeman.com.au

I0601113

Also by Amanda Bridgeman

Aurora Series
#1 Aurora: Darwin
#2 Aurora: Pegasus
#3 Aurora: Meridian
#4 Aurora: Centralis
#5 Aurora: Eden
#6 Aurora: Decima
#7 Aurora: Aurizun
#8 Aurora: Atlas

Salvation Series
#1 The Subjugate
#2 The Sensation

Spud Compton Series
#1 The Darkest Cargo
#2 The Deepest Jungle
#3 The Deftest Deceit

The Time of the Stripes

Pandemic
Patient Zero

Marvel: School of X
Sound of Light

SHORT STORIES

Marvel: School of X anthology
Eye of the Storm

Inferno! Presents: The Emperor's Finest
Reconsecration

THE DARKEST CARGO

SPUD COMPTON #1

AMANDA BRIDGEMAN

COPYRIGHT

The Darkest Cargo
EPUB format: 978-0-6482162-7-8
PRINT format: 978-0-6457363-0-4

Original cover design by
Amanda Pillar of Smoking Hot Covers

CHAPTER ONE

Spud Compton lifted the glass of bourbon to his lips.

"Oh, baby, how I missed you."

Nikita scowled, flicking her long dark braids over her shoulder. "Your fault for booking us a long passage without station stops," she said, before downing her shot of tequila and slamming the glass back on the bar.

"Hey, look, we go where the money is. The client wanted us to do direct, so we did. The station stops would've cost us time," he shrugged. "Besides," he smiled at her, "lucky for us our pilot got us here in good time."

She gave him an unimpressed stare. "You don't pay me enough. One of these days I'm going to leave you."

"For another ship?" He waved her off. "Just try to find a better captain than me."

She kept her stare fixed on his face, her dark eyes a wall of immovable angst.

Spud grinned. "Or another captain that will put up with your moods."

Her stare turned harder.

"Oh, come on, Nik." He knocked her dark-skinned elbow with his own. "Let me buy you another drink." He waved for the bartender.

"So you damn well should," she muttered.

"Seriously, Nik, why are you always so grumpy?"

"Why are you so overly optimistic?"

"See!" he grinned again. "That's why we're a good team, you know. We balance each other out. You pop my balloons and I inflate yours."

Nikita shook her head, braids swinging, as he ordered another round of drinks.

"Where'd the others get to tonight?" he asked.

"Glossy and Finn will be in the casino, no doubt," she said, referring to their engineer and security. "I suspect Miguel is lost in the market buying supplies since you only gave us 24 hours here." She narrowed her eyes. "And I'm pretty sure we don't want to know where King went."

"No," he said, handing her another shot of tequila, "and that's precisely why I only gave us 24 hours here: to stop Glossy and Finn losing all their money, stop Miguel from spending too much of *my* money, stop you from getting into a fight—"

"A fight?" She looked at him like he smelled bad.

"—and to stop King from getting us all arrested."

"Oh, so you're the innocent party here, keeping us all in line, huh?"

"Of course," he said, grinning.

"You do well enough at getting yourself into trouble, chief," she said, downing her shot.

"Only when it comes to women. You're all a menace."

"No, you're just gullible."

"Ouch. That hurt."

"It should. You ought to be ashamed of yourself. You think your cute face and pretty smile will get you out of anything, but the truth is, all it does is attract the vultures. They see you coming from a mile away. Rich, foolish, white boy. You might as well have a big fat target on your back."

"I'm not rich! Have you seen my ship?"

"You would be rich if you just sucked up to your daddy."

"I don't need his money. I'm making my own way just fine, thank you."

Nikita gave him a look of doubt. Spud needed to change the topic of conversation.

"So, Nikita, how long's it been since you had a girlfriend?"

She grunted. "Women are nothing but trouble, Spud." She left her barstool and looked around, wiping her mouth.

"Where're you going?"

"To find me some trouble."

Spud chuckled and shook his head. "Ship leaves at 0800!" he called after her, then turned back to his drink.

Spud ambled down the corridors of New Moon Station with a smile pasted across his face. He was only lightly drunk, but it was a nice place to be. The lighting of the station had softened, set to evening mode, but according to the data-band around his wrist, the hour was only 20:54. It was a little too early to go back to his ship, *Benobi-451*, just yet. Besides, he enjoyed the walk and the fresh surrounds. He stretched his 5'11 frame and nodded politely to a couple of cute women who passed by. They didn't return the gesture. That was one difference he'd noticed of no longer wearing a uniform. The uniform always got the nods and the smiles. Now he was just a regular guy and had somehow slipped a few rungs down the ladder of eligible bachelors. That, and he wasn't quite in the same shape he'd once been, when wearing that uniform. He glanced down at the slight padding across his belly, as fleeting thoughts of getting back into some kind of fitness regime crossed his mind. It's not that he'd lost his fitness, he just wasn't as disciplined about it as he once was. It was kind of the point of his new lifestyle. Freedom.

He pulled into Felix's Bar. It was a favorite on station, a place filled with smooth tunes, sultry singers and old liquor. Dusted in low red lighting and velvet lounges, it felt as far away from a station in space as you could get. In short, it was the perfect place to indulge in a nightcap before he'd have to set sail again and face the endless black.

He took a seat in the corner, ordered a drink with a waiter, then sat back and relaxed. He needed to do this more often, he thought. *Relax.* It was hard right now as he was still trying to build up his cargo running business. Changing career midlife was never going to be easy, and many wanted to see him fail, see him go crawling back to his old life, but it wasn't an option for him. Failure. He'd prove them wrong. He'd prove his father wrong. He was going to build a solid business and maybe one day enjoy more nights like this.

The waiter delivered his drink, and he smiled a thank you.

"To the future, Spud," he said, raising his glass to himself and taking a drink.

It had been a tough few years but he was finally gaining traction. He'd started on his own doing small gigs, then built up the business to employ a crew of five and managed to buy a decent ship. And by decent he meant one that was several decades old, but thanks to Glossy's TLC it ran just fine. The routes were long, the time hard, but he was doing it because no one else was. He'd found a hole in the market and was doing his best to fill it. Take the jobs no one else wants. Reap the rewards.

The data-band on his wrist alerted him to an incoming call. He didn't recognize the number. He contemplated ignoring it, but then... it could be another job and he wasn't in a position to turn any down. He switched the call to his handset, clipped it off his belt.

"Spud Compton," he answered.

"Answering work calls in a bar, Spud? Really?"

He paused a moment, then furrowed his brow. "Shayla?"

"You remember."

"Of course, I remember... We dated for, what, four years?"

"About that."

"Yeah, four years. That was it," he said. "Four whole years before I caught you in bed with Lieutenant Fendel."

"You're still bitter about that?"

He hated how damn sexy her voice was. If she could sing, she'd be giving the sultry singer on stage a run for her money.

"I don't know," Spud said. "Maybe if he'd been the only one, but there was Sergeant Lofts, Captain Wylie. I don't know, I lost count. Do you even know how many it was?"

"What can I say? You were away a lot."

"Doing my duty, Shayla. Being military, you of all people should've understood that."

She gave a bored sigh. "Look, Spud, I didn't call up to apologize. This isn't a personal call. This is business."

"Business?" he chuckled. "What possible business could you have with me?"

"I heard you're running cargo."

"Yeah."

"Then I have some cargo for you to run."

Spud paused, curious. "Well, there's plenty of cargo runners out there, Shayla."

"I need someone I can trust."

He paused again before he burst out laughing.

"Something funny?" she asked.

"Yeah. You talking about trust."

"Jesus, Compton. Put on your big boy shoes for five minutes," she scolded him. "Where's the soldier you used to be?"

"Oh, he's retired," Spud said, taking another sip of his drink.

"The soldier never leaves you," she said. "So find your spine and let's talk business."

"Now, just a minute—"

"Put your drink down and listen!"

Spud paused, looked at the glass in his hand. "How'd you know I was drinking?"

"Wow. You've really lost your surveillance skills, haven't you?"

He glanced around and saw her standing there, phone to her ear. She wore a tight, low-cut dress that accentuated her curves, and her long blond hair rested lazily over her shoulders. He couldn't help but gape back. Even across the dim room he could see her blue eyes piercing his as she smiled. *Goddamn* she looked good... He tore his eyes away from her. This had trouble written all over it.

She sat down in the chair opposite him, hung up on the call.

"What are you doing here?" he asked, putting his phone away.

"I heard you were on station. Thought I'd come and say hello."

"Why?" he asked.

"I told you. I have cargo that needs running and I need someone I can trust."

"Not my problem."

"That's a lot of zeros you're turning down, Spud. No wonder your business hasn't taken off yet."

"My business is doing just fine, thank you," he said, glancing away to the sultry singer on the stage. He took a sip of his drink and looked back to see her smiling at him like she knew a big secret. His mind turned over. "How many zeros are we talking?"

"*Many* zeros."

"What's the cargo?"

"It's classified."

"Military, then."

She gave a single, subtle nod.

"So why doesn't the navy get one of their approved cargo operators to do it?"

"Because this is so classified, it's off the books."

He stared at her. "I'm done with the navy, Shayla. You can't drag me back in."

"I don't want to drag you back in, Spud. I just want to pay you a lot of zeroes to shift some cargo. Imagine what all those zeroes could do for your business."

Spud finished his drink, contemplating the offer.

"I'm going to need more information."

"Well, why don't you buy me a drink and I'll tell you all about it."

"I thought it was classified?"

She didn't answer but stared at him with her best bedroom eyes.

"If you want me to help you," he said, "perhaps *you* should buy *me* a drink."

"Alright," she said, then waved the barman over.

CHAPTER TWO

Spud opened his eyes and slammed his hand against the comms panel on the wall above his bed to kill the alarm. Head aching, mouth a little dry, he rubbed his eyes, then suddenly looked at what lay in the bed next to him.

Shayla. Naked.

"Oh, shit..." he muttered quietly, closing his eyes.

Shayla moved sleepily, snuggling warm against him. He eyed her naked body against his.

God, he was weak.

But damn, she was beautiful.

He checked the time on his data-band.

"Shit," he muttered again, then shook Shayla's shoulder. "Shayla? Shayla, wake up."

She stirred and opened her eyes, giving him that sleepy sex kitten look she did so well. "Morning," she purred.

"Morning," he said, throwing the sheets back and getting out of bed. He glanced back at her as he pulled his trousers up.

"Last night was fun," she smiled.

He pulled on a shirt and tugged on his boots, regret flooding through him. "Yeah. I gotta go prepare the ship for departure."

"Spud," she said. "Everything alright?"

"Yeah," he nodded averting his eyes as moved to the door.

"You sure about that?" she said sitting up and gathering the sheets around her chest. "You know, I can crash elsewhere on the ship for the duration of the trip if you'd prefer it to me staying in here with you."

"I said it's fine." He opened his cabin door, then paused and looked back at her. "Must be some cargo if you need to personally escort it, huh? What'd you say it was again?"

"I didn't. We drank. *A lot.* We reminisced on old times then you brought me back here and..." she beamed a smile. "Just take me to Sailors' Junction, Spud, and you'll get all those zeros. That's all you need to know."

● ● ●

Spud walked into the *Benobi's* small mess and headed straight for the coffee he knew Miguel would've prepped by now. He poured a cup and took a sip, just as something soft hit him in the head. He grabbed at it. It was a black lace bra.

Shayla's black lace bra.

He turned and saw Nikita standing in the doorway.

"I'm not touching the panties. You can find them on the floor in the corner," Nikita pointed. Spud spotted them on the floor, as memories of last night flashed through his mind.

"Oh. Right... Sorry."

"You better get her ass off the ship. We're leaving in 20 minutes."

"No need. She's coming with us."

Nikita fixed him with a firm stare. "What?"

"I picked up another job last night. We're taking her to Sailors' Junction to pick up some cargo, then we're dropping them both off in Vanguard City."

"You picked up another job." She stared at him. "What about our current job?"

"We're still doing that. We're just making a slight detour."

"Slight detour..." Nikita said, as she crossed her slim but muscular arms. "Vanguard City is on the other side of The Wastelands, Spud. That's a long trip."

Spud nodded, averting his eyes and drinking his coffee.

"Spud, what the hell?" she demanded.

"It's paying triple, Nik," he said.

"Triple?! Who's the client?"

"Er... an old friend."

"Who?" Nikita's eyes narrowed in suspicion, fixing him with a razor-sharp stare.

"Er..."

"Spud, have you seen my…?" Shayla entered the mess, wearing his shirt from last night. She saw the bra and plucked it from his hand, then turned to Nikita. "Hi. I'm Shayla." She offered her hand to the pilot.

"Shayla?!" Nikita said, eyes popping white as she looked back at Spud. "Oh, you didn't…"

"Shayla's our new client, Nikita," Spud said quickly, as Shayla dropped her unshaken hand. "She'll be staying on board until we hit Vanguard City." He looked back at Shayla. "Nikita's my pilot," he said, then lowered his voice to a whisper. "Your underwear is in the corner."

"Ah!" she said, then picked them up and headed back to Spud's cabin.

As soon as she'd left the room, Nikita stared at him, eyes filled with exasperation.

Spud cut her off before she could say anything. "She's paying triple, Nik!"

"Was that before or after she gave you the extras?"

Spud would've blushed then if he was the blushing type. "It's just a job."

Nikita shook her head. "Damn, Spud. I thought you had more self-respect than that."

"C'mon Nik…"

The pilot stepped forward and slapped him hard.

Spud groaned and rubbed his cheek. "What the hell was that for?"

Nikita stepped closer. "You told me once, that if you ever hooked up with your ex again, to slap you," she shrugged. "So, I just did."

Spud couldn't really argue with that. "Fair enough."

Nikita slapped him again.

"Jesus!" he said. "And what was that for?!"

"The first one was for you, the second one was from me. That's what friends are for, Spud."

She left the room and Spud sighed. He rubbed his cheek again, then took his mug of coffee and headed to his office.

● ● ●

Spud reentered the *Benobi*'s mess to see the crew gathered. Shayla, now fully dressed, was by his side.

"Folks, this here's Shayla Morrison," he said. "We're transporting her to collect some cargo at Sailor's Junction, then dropping them off at Vanguard City, so she'll be with us for the duration." Spud glanced at her. "Shayla, this is my crew." He motioned to King, leaning his tall, lean frame against the wall, blue eyes curious beneath a blond crewcut. "This here's King, he's our medical officer," Spud told her. King gave Shayla a nod but said nothing. Spud then motioned to Glossy. She stood beside King, her small, stocky frame barely reaching King's shoulders; her heavily tattooed arms folded across her chest. "This is Glossy. She's our engineer." Shayla gave a nod and Glossy stared back, mute, her dark Latina eyes analyzing beneath a crop of bright pink hair shaved close to her skull. Spud moved on, motioning to the eldest member of his crew, wearing a dirty apron. "This is Miguel. He keeps us fed and watered." Miguel gave Shayla a nod with appraising eyes as he scratched his stubbled jaw. "And lastly," Spud said, motioning to Finn, tall, athletic, dark-haired, standing with his hands on his hips, "This is Finn. He's my security officer."

Finn gave a short sharp laugh. "That's nice of you to call me that, Spud. What he means is, I'm the grunt who does all the work."

"Security grunt," Spud smiled.

"You need a bodyguard, Spud?" Shayla smiled at him. "Is that because you're important now? Or have you just gotten so lazy you can't take care of yourself anymore?"

The room was silent, waiting for his response.

"I can take care of myself just fine," he said. "But we have a lot of cargo to protect and a second pair of hands doesn't go astray."

"A second pair of hands?" she said, then glanced at his crew. "I see more hands than that. You're all ex-military, am I right?"

They stared back at her, appearing a little surprised she'd guessed it right.

"It takes one to know one," Shayla smiled.

"You're ex-military?" Finn asked.

"No. I'm still serving. I know what military looks like." She glanced at Spud. "And I know Spud. He claims to have left the navy behind, but there's no way that'll ever happen."

"Yeah, why's that?" King asked.

Shayla shot Spud a curious look at King's question.

"Shayla's wishful thinking," Spud said quickly.

That smile crept across Shayla's mouth again like she knew a secret. Only this time he knew she did. No one else, other than Nikita, knew who Spud's father was. *Or,* who his brother was.

"I'm sure the navy would welcome you back with open arms," Shayla told Spud with a sly smile. "Just like family."

"No, they won't, because I was medically discharged." He tapped his thigh, referring to a bullet wound he'd received. "Now prep for departure. We leave in ten."

And he swiftly left the room.

● ● ●

Spud looked up at the knock on the door of his small, cramped office. Miguel stood there.

"I know what you're going to say, Miguel—"

"I have another mouth to feed."

"She's paying triple, Miguel. You can buy more at Sailors' Junction."

"Triple?" he quirked an eyebrow curiously.

Spud nodded. "If anyone can make that food stretch to feed another mouth, it's you, my friend."

"Of course I can," Miguel grunted. "I fed a team of ten for almost five weeks when we were trapped under rubble in the Caskade explosion."

"I know. That's why you're my man."

Miguel grunted again. "Well... if we run short, I suppose I can serve up your balls, given Shayla's already cut them off."

"What?" Spud said, then pointed at him. "Don't listen to what Nik says."

Finn stuck his head around the doorway with a grin pasted on his face. "I wouldn't say she's cut them off, Miguel. I'd just say she's holding them real tight." He held up his clenched fist. "But one false move and she'll twist them right off."

"Hey, that's not true!" Spud said offended.

King appeared in the crowded doorway next. "It's alright, I'll prep the med room for emergency surgery. If it comes to that I might be able to sew them back on."

Spud gave a sarcastic grin. "Look, if you guys don't want the triple payment, I'm happy to keep that for myself."

"Triple?" King blinked.

"Yes," Spud said, leaning forward over his desk. "And that's the kind of captain I am. I'm taking a hit for my team."

Finn laughed. "Taking a hit? Is that what you call it?"

"There's worse ways to go," King said. "She's a fine-looking specimen."

Miguel raised a clenched fist, shaking it. "And she knows she's got him."

The three men were suddenly shoved aside as Glossy came to stand in the doorway. "If you're done?" she said to the three crewmen, before looking at Spud. "Where are we fitting this cargo? How big is it?"

"She says it's one large box. We'll find room."

"How heavy?" Glossy asked, staring at him, unimpressed.

"We'll find out when we get to Sailors' Junction."

She folded her tattooed arms, the skulls on her forearms glaring at Spud in support of Glossy's face. She shook her head and walked away, muttering, "Unbelievable."

Spud eyed the now empty doorway and sighed, rubbing his tired face, and trying to wipe away his hangover.

● ● ●

With the *Benobi* well on its way to Sailor's Junction, the crew sat around the mess table with Shayla, enjoying a dinner of Miguel's best goulash.

"Mmm. This is good," Shayla told him.

Miguel grunted. "Of course it's good. I made it."

"What kind of spice did you put in it?"

Miguel stared at her. "I'll never tell."

"Well, he could," Finn said, "but then he'd have to kill you."

"And that would just be messy," King added.

"Heaven forbid you actually have to work, now," Glossy chided him.

"Hey, I work!" King said.

"When?" Glossy argued. "We never get sick."

"That's because I take good care of you."

"Pffft!" Glossy blew him off.

"You ever work the frontlines?" Shayla asked King.

He finished his mouthful of goulash, averting his eyes. "Yeah. I did my time."

"Yeah? Which war?"

King's eyes returned to hers as the mess fell silent. "Does it matter?"

"Just making conversation," she shrugged. "Some soldiers see a lot, and some see next to nothing."

King gave a small smile, stirred his bowl for a moment, then stood. He mumbled something about sorting out supplies, then picked up his bowl and left the mess. Spud's shoulders slumped as he watched him leave.

"Something I said?" she asked.

Spud looked at her. "You heard about Daridian Station?"

"Daridian Station?" she said. "Yeah. Who hasn't? That was that bloodbath where the station's governor had most of his civilians slaughtered."

Spud nodded. "King was on the first ship that arrived afterward. It was his job to clean up the bodies and save who he could. There weren't many to save. Children, babies… murdered in cold blood."

"That must've been a helluva thing to see," Shayla said quietly.

"It was," Nikita said, bluntly. "Enough to make it the last job he ever did with the navy." She too picked up her bowl and left the mess.

"I don't think she likes me," Shayla said nonchalantly.

Silence was her response.

"So, what about you?" Glossy asked. "What are your credentials?"

"My credentials?" Shayla chuckled.

"Well, you seem to want to know ours." Glossy gave a fake smile.

"Who I work for is irrelevant."

"But you worked with Spud once, right?" Finn asked.

"I did," she nodded. "For a time. Then he transferred units. After that he was never around much."

"I went where I was told to go," Spud defended himself. "I was assigned to the *Katoma*, so when it sailed, so did I."

Shayla laughed. "You could've taken a base posting any time, Spud. You chose to roam… And then you wondered why I did."

Silence filled the mess again, but the expressions on the faces of Spud's crew were loud and clear. They looked at him for his response; waited for his response.

Spud glanced at her, then shrugged. "I was a military man, Shayla. I expected loyalty."

And with that, he too grabbed his plate and left the room.

CHAPTER THREE

Shayla knocked quietly on the door to Spud's cabin. Laying on his bunk, reading, he looked up from the device he was holding.

"Am I allowed in?" she asked.

Spud said nothing but motioned her in with a wave of his hand.

"I'm sorry for the dig at dinner," she said.

"You haven't paid me yet," Spud said. "I checked."

Shayla looked at her data-band. "You'll be paid as soon as I am."

"And when is that?"

"In a few hours."

"That wasn't our deal. Half up front, half on delivery."

She came to sit on the side of his bed. "You'll get it, Spud." She reached out and placed a hand on his arm. He shrugged it off.

"If I don't, I'll be unloading you at the nearest station."

"I said, you'll get it."

He tossed the device aside and moved to get out of bed.

"Spud," she placed her hands on his chest to stop him. "I'm sorry alright. Don't be like this."

"Like what?" he said, pushing past her hands and standing.

"A bitter teenager."

"A bitter teenager?" Spud chuckled and shook his head. "God... I honestly don't know what I ever saw in you."

Shayla smiled. "Yes, you do. When we first got together we didn't leave the bedroom for days." She tried her sex kitten eyes on him again.

"Well, I was young and dumb back then. Things have changed." He moved toward the door.

"If things have changed, why haven't you moved on, Spud? Why are you still single?"

"Why are *you* still single?" He shot back as he reached the cabin door. "I may be single, Shayla, but I've got my crew and they're my family. What have you got? Nothing. There's a reason for that."

With that, Spud left the cabin and stomped down the corridor.

● ● ●

Spud knocked on the door to King's cabin. A few moments passed before it opened a crack and a blue eye stared out at him. Spud noticed King's eye seemed glassy, vague.

"I just wanted to stop by and check on you," Spud said, studying him.

"I'm fine."

"Forget Shayla. She's good at... well, she's good at making people feel like shit."

King continued to stare at him through the crack.

"Can I come in?" Spud asked.

"No. I'm fine."

Spud pushed the door open, and King sighed.

"I haven't touched anything," King said quickly upon Spud seeing the bottle of vodka and a syringe and vial close by.

Spud looked back at him.

"I'm just testing myself," King said, sitting down on his bunk. "It's what I do. I just stare at it and think about all the things I've messed up in my life. It reminds me not to go there again. The syringe is still in its package."

"It's an interesting way to handle it," Spud said picking up the bottle. "You pick this up on New Moon Station?"

King nodded, then shrugged. "You threw out my last bottle."

"I did," Spud said, "and I'm going to have to take this one too."

"Spud—"

"You know my rules, King. That's why you're here. 'Cause I don't allow drugs or booze on board my ship."

King sighed. "I know."

Spud swiped the syringe and vial and placed them in his trouser pocket. "You've been doing well, man. I'm not going to let you blow it. Alright?"

King nodded.

"You work on my ship, I help you dry out. That's the deal." Spud reached out and squeezed his shoulder. "I'm here for you, man."

King gave Spud's arm a friendly punch. "I'm here for you, too."

Spud gave a smile, picked up the bottle of booze, then headed for the door.

"Spud?" King stopped him.

"Yeah?"

"Thanks… for helping me."

"That's alright."

"If I could take Shayla away from you, I would."

Spud furrowed his brow.

King shrugged. "We've all got our vices. I've got my drugs and booze, and you've got her."

"She's not a problem."

"Isn't she?"

"No. As soon as we hit Vanguard City, she's gone from my life for good."

The look King gave him lacked belief.

"I mean it," Spud said firmly.

"Denial is the first step to overcome," King said quietly.

Spud eyed him, then glanced around the room and left.

● ● ●

"We're on approach to Sailor's Junction," Nikita's voice sounded over the ship's speakers.

"Roger that," Spud spoke into the comms panel in his office. "On my way to the flight deck." He downed what was left of his coffee, then stepped into the corridor.

It had been a relatively subdued four days' journey to Sailor's Junction, located on the border of the area known as The Wastelands. Basically, from this point forward until they hit Vanguard City there were no other stations and few who cared to travel the distance. Except Spud and the *Benobi*, of course. It was a lonely journey to Vanguard City, and Spud was starting to think it would be his loneliest yet. Over the past four days, the crew had been keeping their distance from him and Shayla, their behavior cautious with the guest on board. Whether it was because they knew she was his ex-girlfriend—God knows what Nikita had told them—and that things were tense, or whether it was because she was navy, Spud didn't know. He had to admit, though, he was looking forward to getting her off his ship. The way the crew had goaded him about being weak and giving into her, had gotten to him. And Nikita's slap still stung his cheek. In fact, that's what bothered him the most. Nik had barely said a word to him these past few days. Nik was his best friend, so her scorn burned him bad.

That, and the fact that she was right.

As hard as it had been, he'd maintained his restraint and hadn't slept with Shayla again, despite her sharing his bed and trying to snuggle with him during the night. When she had, he'd simply moved her away and rolled over. He didn't like being a fool, and being with her, he was a huge one. She'd always played him, used him, and he'd let her. When he'd finally broken up with her all those years ago, he'd sworn he would never let himself get caught up with her again. Yet, here he was.

Nikita should've punched him.

Still, Shayla was paying triple and he needed that right now. He just wanted to pick up this cargo and get it to wherever it was going as fast as he could, so he could dump the both of them off his ship. He'd survived so far. He just had one leg of the journey left to go.

● ● ●

He entered the *Benobi*'s small flight deck, where Nikita sat alone at the desk.

"Sailor's Junction…" Nikita glanced at him as he sat in the spare seat beside her, then continued into her comms mic, "this is *Benobi-451* requesting permission to dock."

"*Benobi-451*, this is Sailor's Junction. Permission granted. Make your way to Bay 77. Repeat, Bay 77."

"Roger that," Nikita said, then ended the comms.

Shayla entered the flight deck. "Everything good?"

"Yeah," Spud nodded. "How many bodies do you need to collect the cargo?"

"I'll handle it myself."

"You sure?"

"Yeah. I'm quite capable, Spud."

"Alright. I'll tell the others, they can have a night off."

"A night off?" Shayla said sharply.

"Yeah. Crossing The Wastelands is quite a stretch. It's a long time between stations. It's important to let the crew off the ship when we can."

"I'd prefer we load the cargo and continue on. I have a deadline to meet."

Spud looked at her. "Well, Miguel needs to get some more supplies, so we have to stop for a bit."

"Tell him he's got an hour."

Spud stared at her. She smiled back and shrugged. "I'm the paying customer, Spud. We load the cargo and go."

Shayla left the flight deck and Nikita stared at him.

He raised his hand. "Don't say a word, Nik."

"I've seen you tackle 300-pound men to the ground, and yet you can't say no to her."

"She's the paying customer," Spud said standing and moving to the door.

"She's your kryptonite, Spud," Nikita muttered after him.

He threw her a glance but left without another word.

● ● ●

Spud watched as Shayla wheeled the large metal box onto the *Benobi*. It was about two meters long, about half that wide, and as high as Spud's waist. The silver casing looked to be a high-tech metal alloy. Whatever it was, it looked expensive. Important. He wondered what it contained.

"So where do you want it?" Glossy asked, taking it from Shayla as Finn stepped up beside her to help.

"Wherever you can fit it," Spud shrugged. The cargo hold wasn't full, but it still held stacks of wooden, plastic and other metal crates along three of the walls, leaving space for the outer bay doors and Glossy's workstation which sat by the door into the *Benobi's* corridor. The floor space in the middle of the hold was clear to allow movement of the cargo when they had to load and unload.

"It needs a steady position, in a corner," Shayla told them, "with no chance of movement."

The three *Benobi* crew looked at her.

"I'm told it's delicate and needs to be kept still," Shayla said. "Treat it as highly fragile."

"Fragile, huh?" Glossy eyed her. "What's inside?"

Shayla smiled at her. "I'm paying triple for a speedy service and no questions."

"Speaking of which," Spud said, "I believe our terms were half up front and half on delivery."

"You'll get it," she said.

"I want it now, Shayla," he said firmly.

She eyed him, then smiled. "You'll have it in your account by tonight."

As she walked off, Glossy and Finn turned to stare at him.

"She hasn't paid us yet?" Glossy asked.

"You heard her," Spud said, unable to hide how pissed he was. "Put it somewhere solid and lock it in."

CHAPTER FOUR

With the *Benobi* crossing The Wastelands and well on the way to Vanguard City, the crew began piling into the small mess for another dinner. This time Miguel served up his tasty chicken casserole.

"Smells good, Mig," Spud said, grabbing a plate.

"It does." Shayla appeared beside him. She knocked her elbow with his. "Check your account, Spud. First half is locked away."

He looked at her, then gave a nod.

"So what are you going to do with all the money?" she asked, as they sat down at the table with their plates. "Give the ship a few upgrades?"

"There's nothing wrong with the ship," Spud said, defensively.

"Sure, if you were living a few decades ago."

Spud ignored her and began eating.

"An overhaul of the engine room wouldn't go astray," Glossy said, darting her eyes to Spud hopefully.

"Yeah, but if you didn't have to fix things, then you'd have nothing to do," King teased her.

"Yeah, like you," she retorted with a sly grin.

"Why don't you just ask your father for some money, Spud?" Shayla asked.

The *Benobi* crew looked at him curiously.

"I'm doing just fine on my own," he said, ignoring their looks.

"Yeah, but you could do so much better if you just dropped your stubbornness and reached out to him."

"Who's your father?" Miguel asked.

Spud looked down at his plate. "No one worth mentioning."

"Spud's doing fine on his own," Nikita spoke up. "He built all this from nothing."

Spud looked at Nik across the table and gave her a grateful look.

"Still," Shayla said, "your family name could open a lot more doors for you."

"Compton?" Finn said, mentally searching for possibilities.

"So, Shayla," Spud said, pulling the comms pane on the table toward him and tapping at it, keen to change the topic of conversation, "when did you say you paid us the first half?"

"Today. As soon as I got paid my first half you got yours."

"Oh, there it is! So, you are a woman of your word."

"I am," she said with a twinkle in her eye. "If I say I'm going to give it to you, you're going to get it."

Finn nearly choked on his food.

"Well, I can't wait until we reach Vanguard City and get the other half," Spud said. "As much as it will be a shame to see you go."

● ● ●

Spud entered the cargo hold to see Glossy standing at her work table by the door, inspecting some ship parts.

"Hey," she said.

"Hey."

"What's up?" she asked.

"Nothing. Just felt like a walk," he said, looking over at Shayla's metal box, gleaming silver where Glossy and Finn had wedged it between an array of stacks of wooden, plastic and other metal crates along the wall to the left. "What're you doing?"

"Maintenance. Making sure our spares are ready to go. I wasn't kidding when I said this ship needs an overhaul. The parts aren't lasting as long as they should."

Spud nodded. "I know. We'll use this money to do that."

He moved his eyes back to Shayla's box. Glossy's eyes followed.

"She tell you what's inside?" she asked.

"No. I'm not sure we want to know."

"It's pretty high-tech, the box," Glossy said. "I can't see any way to open it."

Spud looked at her.

She shrugged. "I was curious."

"Don't try and open it, Gloss. Don't go anywhere near it. Don't even look at it. If it's navy and Shayla's being all mysterious about it, I don't think we want to know."

She nodded, eyeing him carefully. "I can't believe you're back together with her."

"I'm not," he said.

"She's sleeping in your room, Spud."

He shrugged. "There were no other beds for her."

"Right," Glossy said skeptically.

"Hey, she leaves when we hit Vanguard City and we'll never see her again."

Glossy studied him. "She's pretty hot, though."

Spud shrugged. "I don't know. She's not as hot as I once thought she was."

Glossy smirked. "The ugliness inside shines through eventually."

Spud smiled back. "That it does."

"Well, good. I hate to see her treat you like that, Cap." She punched his shoulder. "You're like a brother to me, you know?"

Spud threw his arm around her shoulders and squeezed her to his side. "And you're like a kid sister to me, Gloss." He ran his hand over the pink stubble on her skull.

"Sister from another mister," she smiled.

"That's it," he smiled back, then checked his data-band and sighed. "Alright. I'm gonna go turn in." As he walked out the door he called over his shoulder.

"Stay away from the box!"

● ● ●

Spud stepped out of his shower, towel wrapped around his waist, to see Shayla laying on his bed. She eyed him over and smiled.

"You interested in some fun for old times' sake?"

He considered her a moment. "No, thanks," he said definitively, grabbing some clothes and moving back to his bathroom.

"Only when you're drunk, huh?"

"Something like that."

"I should get you drunk then."

"No drinking allowed on my ship."

"Oh yeah? So why do you have a bottle in your drawer?"

He stopped. "You've been going through my drawers?"

Her smile fell. "And what's with that syringe, Spud. Don't tell me you…"

"It's not mine."

She stared at him.

"I'm just holding it for someone else."

"Right."

"It's not mine," he said firmly.

"Well, I don't see any track marks," she said studying his arms and legs.

"No, you don't. Because it's not mine. You see, when I speak, Shayla, I speak the truth. I know that's an alien concept to you."

"I can too, Spud," she said quietly. "I did love you once, you know. I never lied about that... And the truth is, I've never found another man that's treated me as good as you did. I know I screwed up with you... and when this job came up, honestly, I kind of saw it as a good reason to reconnect with you."

Spud stared at her laying on his bed.

"I figured you could use the money," she said, dripping with vulnerability, "knew you'd help me out, and... I wanted to reconnect."

Spud's eyes dropped to the floor, as thoughts of Nikita, King and Glossy swirled in his mind, as did thoughts of Finn and Miguel clenching their fists... he shook his head. "You burned that bridge, Shayla," he said softly. "You can't cross back over."

"We could build another one? Together."

He eyed her as she pulled off her shirt and patted the bed next to her. He stared at her naked form.

"Nah," he shook his head again. "I'm in a different place now."

And with that, he went back into the bathroom and closed the door.

● ● ●

Spud awoke to an alert sounding over the comms panel above his bed.

"Yeah?" he answered in a rough voice, before noticing Shayla standing fully dressed beside his bed.

"Spud," Nikita's voice sounded. "We've got an unidentified ship on approach."

"How far out?"

"Twenty miles. Its trajectory is headed straight for us and it's slowing down."

"Maybe it's turning?"

"It's not turning," Shayla said. "It's for me."

Spud looked at her through sleep-crusted eyes. "For you?"

Shayla nodded. "Sorry, Spud. It was a secret rendezvous I couldn't tell you about. Not until I knew it was going ahead."

"What?" he asked.

"Nikita!" Shayla called to the comms panel. "I'm coming up to the flight deck. Let me speak with them." She looked at Spud. "Vanguard City was never the cargo's destination, Spud. This approaching ship is."

CHAPTER FIVE

Spud hastily dressed and followed Shayla up the corridor.

"What's going on?" Finn asked as he emerged from his cabin.

Spud glanced around at him. "I don't know."

"You want me on guns?" Finn asked.

"Not yet," Spud said. "Apparently Shayla's expecting them."

Finn narrowed his eyes, but Spud looked away.

They entered the flight deck, as Shayla made herself at home in the chair beside Nikita.

"Can you connect me to their ship?" she asked the *Benobi's* pilot.

Nikita gave her a flat stare.

"Channel DX19," Shayla ordered. "Quickly."

Nikita raised her brows at Shayla, then looked up at Spud.

"Shayla, what the hell is going on?" he asked her.

"Relax. You're still dropping me off at Vanguard City," Shayla said, "but I part ways with the cargo here."

"We're in the middle of nowhere."

"Exactly. Now hook me up to their comms."

"Not until you tell me what's going on," Spud said.

"I told you, it's classified." She glared at him. "Now hook me up, so I can shift this cargo. *Stat.*"

Spud stared at her a moment. "Why aren't we doing the exchange at a station? Why out here in The Wastelands?"

"'Because it's classified, Spud! There're no eyes out here."

"It's not navy, is it," Finn, now standing behind Spud, asked, although it was more of a statement. "If it was black ops they'd be using their own crew. Not ours. Not civilians."

A thought suddenly dawned on Spud and he lowered his face, closing his eyes briefly. He looked up again. "It's not classified is it, Shayla? It's goddamned *hot!*"

Shayla ignored him, grabbing a comms headset and pulling it on.

"Why are we dropping off mid-space, Shayla?" Spud demanded. "You don't want eyes seeing what you're doing, because it's illegal, isn't it? *Shit!*" he hissed and leaned toward her. "Please tell me you're not stealing from the navy?"

Shayla threw him a fierce glare. "Spud, if we don't communicate with this ship, it's going to have serious implications for you and your crew."

Spud exchanged a look with Finn, then turned back to Shayla. "I think you're forgetting whose ship you're on here."

"And I think you're forgetting who's paying you," she shot back. "You wanna know how I can afford to pay you triple rates, Spud? These guys," she pointed to the blip showing on the ship's radar. "And I'll tell you, if these guys pay a lot of money for something and then don't get it? You'll all be missing kneecaps, if not more, before the hour is up." She looked back at Nikita. "So hook up the damn comms, *now*."

"Not until you tell me what you're doing," Spud said through clenched teeth.

"Spud, I'm warning you!"

"And I'm warning *you*!"

Shayla exhaled heavily in frustration. "Goddamn it! *Alright!* Have you heard of the Guantano Clan?"

"Guantano Clan?" Finn said. "The mobsters?"

"Yeah," Shayla said. "The ship coming for us, is theirs. And they want their cargo, Spud. That's why they paid so much. Now, if we don't hand it over, they will come and take it anyway and butcher us all."

"How the hell did you get messed up with the Guantano Clan?" Spud asked her.

"It doesn't matter. Look, this isn't a big deal, Spud. Just transfer the goods, then drop me at Vanguard City and we're done."

"Isn't a big deal?!" Nikita said. "You stole from the navy and got us messed up with the Guantano Clan, and you think it's not a big deal?"

"We're not messed up with them until we mess up. So don't mess up!"

"Fuck," Spud muttered, shaking his head.

"We're running out of time, Spud," she said. "Shift the cargo, earn your money, end of story." She adjusted her comms piece and glared at Nikita. "Channel DX19, *please*."

Nikita glanced back at Spud. He eyed the radar blip, then gave Nikita a reluctant nod. Nikita's hands danced around the console before motioning for Shayla to speak.

"*Benobi-451* to *Palomar*," Shayla said. "Do you read, over?"

A few seconds passed before the reply came.

"*Palomar* reading, over. Your silence had us worried for a moment there. Are you ready to dance?"

"No need to be worried. *Benobi* is dressed for the ball and ready to dance. Over," Shayla replied.

"Affirmative. *Palomar* preparing to dance."

Shayla glanced at Nikita. "Prepare to accept transfer cables, we're sending the cargo across to them."

"I thought you said it was fragile?" Finn said. "Isn't that risky?"

"It'll be fine. It's just for a few minutes."

Spud looked at her. "What's in the cargo, Shayla?"

"Spud, it doesn't matter. All that matters is that this *is* happening. *Now*. If you want your money, if you want to make it out of this in one piece, you help me get that cargo off your ship."

"What the hell have you gotten me into?"

"Something you can get yourself out of if you just find your spine! Now prepare to transfer the cargo off your ship!"

Spud shook his head, unable to hide the anger in his eyes. "With pleasure." He looked back at Nikita. "Wake the crew."

● ● ●

While Nikita slowed the ship but continued on course, down in the cargo hold, Spud and Finn, along with Glossy who'd joined them, unlocked the wheels of the metal box and began to pull it out from its secure position against the wall. Dressed in their space suits, they rolled the heavy box toward the sealed door of the cargo hold, ready to move it through to the outer loading bay, where they would depressurize the cabin and then hook it up to the transfer cables sent from the other ship. Once connected, the crate would transfer between ships, mid-space, by the cables' pulley system.

"She's paid you already for this, right?" Glossy asked.

Spud was in a foul mood. He didn't want to discuss it.

"Spud?" Glossy pushed.

"Half!" he spat. "We get the other half when we drop her off."

"Let's drop her off now," Glossy seethed.

"I wish we could," he said darkly, as they reached the door to the outer bay.

"I can't believe you messed us up with the Guantano Clan," Glossy shook her head.

"Glossy!" Finn said firmly. "He understands. Drop it and let's get this done."

An alarm suddenly sounded over their suit comms.

"Spud?" they heard Nikita's voice. "We've got a problem."

"What is it?" Spud asked.

"Another ship. It's approaching fast."

"Shayla?" Spud called into the comms. "Are you expecting this?"

Silence was his reply.

"Shayla?" he repeated. "What's going on?"

"Oh, *shit*," Nikita said. "It's navy."

"Navy!"

"It's a small vessel, but it's still navy, Spud, and it's headed our way."

"Shayla?" he questioned.

"Hurry!" Shayla barked over the comms. "We need to get the cargo onto the other ship, now!"

"Why the hell are the navy here, Shayla?" Spud demanded.

"Why do you think? Now move!"

"I thought you had this under control? I thought this was the easiest money I'd ever make."

"Move the cargo now, and it won't be your problem."

"Except that a navy ship is on approach about to witness the transfer!"

"We can't do it," Glossy said, stepping back from the container.

"We can't get caught with stolen goods either," Finn told her.

"It's too late," Spud said. "We already have."

"If I mess up again, I'm gone, Spud," Glossy said, concerned. "I ain't going to jail."

"Just move the cargo now!" Shayla barked. "It's face the navy or face the Guantano Clan. I know which one I'd rather choose."

The flight deck comms sounded over their earpieces.

"Vessel *Benobi-451*, this is Galactic Navy vessel *Saputra*," a woman's voice announced. "Disengage all weapons and prepare for boarding. I repeat. Disengage all weapons and prepare for boarding. Do you understand my order?"

The silence sat as Spud's mind raced.

"What should I tell them?" Nikita's voice sounded over their comms.

Spud watched as Glossy wrapped her arms over her head and began to pace.

"Shit!" Shayla said. "Shit, shit, *shit!*"

"What?" Spud called.

"The Guantano ship is changing course," Nikita said.

The voice of the navy officer sounded again. "Vessel *Palomar*, this is Galactic Navy vessel *Saputra*. We command you to stop. I repeat, we command you stop or we will be forced to fire."

Another alarm could be heard sounding from the flight deck console.

"Jesus!" Nikita gasped. "The Guantano ship is burning hot! They're gonna fire on the goddamn navy!"

"They what?" Finn's eyes popped as Glossy looked up.

"Navy's burning up too!" Nikita added.

"Get out of the way!" Spud barked. "Get us out of the way! *Now!*"

"What do you think I'm doing!" Nikita snapped back.

Spud felt the *Benobi* suddenly veer hard to the right and they all lost their feet. The cargo flew out of their grasp and smacked violently into the bay door, bouncing back off it. Finn quickly sprang to his feet and threw his arms over it, to stop its movement.

"It's okay!" he panted. "I got it!"

"What do we do?" Glossy asked getting to her feet. "What do we do?"

"Nik, what's happening?" Spud asked, standing, as a vibration suddenly shook the ship.

"They fired!" Nikita exclaimed. "They fired on the goddamn navy!"

"Did they hit?" Spud asked.

"No. Missed. But the navy's targeting back."

"Are we clear?"

"Yes, I'm moving us! I'm moving us!"

"Not too far!" Spud barked. "We don't want the navy thinking we're running!"

"Roger that!"

"No!" Shayla said. "We need to run. We can rendezvous with them somewhere else."

"Are you kidding me?!" Spud exclaimed.

"You don't understand, Spud," Shayla said.

"No, I don't think *you* understand, Shayla. The navy is about to kick down our goddamn door!"

"The navy is the least of our problems, Spud. If we don't deliver this cargo to the Guantano Clan—"

"Shit," Finn said staring down at the cargo.

Spud and Glossy looked at him.

"What?" Spud asked.

Finn pressed his ear against the lid. "I can hear something hissing inside. Something must've come loose when it crashed against the wall."

"What's in the cargo, Shayla?" Spud asked.

"I don't know."

"Is it a weapon? Can it blow up my ship?"

"I don't know!"

"*Palomar* is firing again!" Nikita yelled.

The ship shuddered and swerved on a tight angle again, and the container with it. It ripped free of Finn's hands and slammed into the wall of crates and bounced off again, loosening other boxes and sending a couple tumbling down. Spud and Glossy threw themselves against it, followed by Finn, fighting to keep it steady as it rolled this way and that on its wheels.

"We can outrun that navy ship, Spud!" Shayla barked. "We can rendezvous with the Clan elsewhere."

"No, Shayla!" Spud yelled. "We're not running anywhere. That navy ship will blow us out of the skies. And if they don't, they'll bring in another ship that can."

"Not if we run fast!"

"Spud, maybe—?" Glossy began.

"No, Glossy," Spud said, firmly. "I promise I won't let anything happen to you."

"We run. *Now!*" Shayla seethed over the comms.

"Oh, bitch, please!" Nikita spat. "You did *not* just pull a gun on me!"

"She what?" Spud said into his helmet comms. "Drop the gun, Shayla!"

"Get us out of here, now!" Shayla yelled at Nikita.

"This is *my* ship, Shayla!" Spud yelled back. "And I say we take our chances with the navy. *Drop the gun!*"

Another shudder rumbled through the ship, it lurched, and yet again the container ripped free of their hands and slammed hard against the wall. The three of them threw themselves atop it once more, but this time, the container banged back at them.

"Whoa!" Finn said, as all three pulled back, startled. "Did you see that?"

"Drop the gun," they heard King's voice sound over their comms.

"You're outnumbered," Miguel's voice backed him up. "Do it."

"Spud, we need to run!" Shayla begged. "We can do it!"

They heard the sound of a scuffle, then a thud.

"Raise a gun to *me*, bitch!" Nikita hissed.

"What the hell just happened?" Spud called out.

"Nikita knocked your girlfriend out," King told him.

"*EX*-girlfriend," Spud clarified. "Nik, I owe you a drink."

"You owe me more than that," she replied.

Another shudder vibrated through the ship and the container began to move. Spud and his two crew pushed it back against the wall. Finn pressed his ear to it again.

"It's still hissing," he said. "Something's leaking inside. This isn't good, Spud."

"That movement before," Glossy said, "something must've popped or burst inside."

"Nikita, what's happening?" Spud asked.

"They're firing back and forth, but it looks like the *Palomar* is running."

"King!" Spud said. "Wake Shayla up. We need to know what's inside this box."

"On it," King called back.

"*Palomar* is still running but the navy aren't chasing," Nikita said. "Looks like they're coming for us instead."

"Alright," Spud said. "Take it easy. Disengage all weapons. Let's look nice and friendly, huh?"

He heard Shayla begin to stir over their comms.

"Screw the smelling salts," Nikita said, before a slap sounded, then more scuffling.

"Break it up you two!" King said.

"The navy is about to be on our doorstep," Nikita reported.

"God, they're going to kill us all," Shayla muttered.

"No," Spud said, "the Guantano Clan is only going to kill you, Shayla."

"I'm not talking about them, Spud!"

"The navy won't kill us," Spud said. "Not if we give them what they want."

"You don't understand, Spud," Shayla said. "The cargo I stole, it originated from Quadrant Four."

"What's Quadrant Four?" Glossy asked.

"Oh, shit..." Finn said, stepping back from the box.

"What's Quadrant Four?" Spud asked him.

"Black ops," Finn answered, fear dripping from his voice as he stared at the box. "So black, few know about it."

"How do you know then?" Glossy asked.

"We all have a past, Glossy. Black ops was mine." Finn locked eyes with Spud. "This isn't good, Spud." He turned back to the cargo. "What's in the cargo, Shayla?"

"I don't know," Shayla's voice sounded.

"You must," Spud said. "Stop lying!"

"I'm not lying! I don't know! All I had to do was transfer the cargo to this position and hand it over. I didn't ask questions."

"Which sector of Quadrant Four did it come from?" Finn asked.

"I don't know!"

"Is it something biological?" Finn asked. "Is it weaponry? Is this thing going to blow or what?"

"I don't know!"

"You said it was fragile," Finn said. "That must mean it's a weapon, right? A bomb?"

"I said I don't know. I was paid not to ask questions."

"Jesus, Shayla," Spud said, "and you thought I was dumb!"

"Don't ask, don't tell," she said. "You know how it goes, Spud."

More instructions sounded over their earpieces.

"Vessel *Benobi-451*. This is Galactic Navy vessel *Saputra*. Prepare for boarding. If you attempt to run we will be forced to stop you. Do you understand?"

"What do we do, Spud?" Nikita asked.

Spud looked at the box, then at the concerned faces of Finn and Glossy. "Tell the navy we grant them permission to board. I don't care what's in this box. I just want it the hell off my ship."

"Spud, please!" Shayla said. "They're going to lock me up."

He stared at the box. "You should've thought of that before, Shayla. I'm not helping you out of this. Nik, tell them to chill out and lower their weapons. They can board anytime they like."

CHAPTER SIX

Spud, Finn and Glossy stood by the sealed door to the cargo hold in their space suits, waiting for Nikita to confirm the small navy tender ship was attached and the pressure balance of the outer bay was complete. Glossy was agitated with nerves, but Spud reached out and gently squeezed her shoulder.

"It's gonna be alright. Relax."

Upon receiving confirmation that the pressurization process was complete and the navy were now in the sealed outer bay, Spud had Finn disengage the door and they stepped back. When the hatch opened, they saw six soldiers: five men and one woman, all armed. Their large automatic stun weapons were aimed at Spud and his crew. Spud had never been hit by a stunner, but he'd seen others hit by one. The darts they fired dug into the flesh and sent an electrical charge through the nervous system that locked the body up. It was clean, but painful and utterly incapacitating, if only for a few minutes.

Spud held up his hands calmly. "We're unarmed!"

"Turn around!" the woman yelled as they stepped into the cargo hold. "On your knees and place your hands on your head!" He recognized her voice as the one who'd spoken over the comms earlier.

"Alright." Spud gave Finn and Glossy a nod to comply. They did so, turning around and kneeling. "If you've looked up my ship," Spud said carefully, placing his hands on his head, "then you'll know we're just a cargo runner. Whatever is going on here, we weren't a part of it."

"Go round up the others," the woman ordered three of her team, who exited the cargo hold into the corridor. "You weren't a part of it?" the female soldier asked Spud, moving to stand in front of him. She lowered her weapon as the remaining two soldiers continued their coverage. The name on her uniform said "Eve Grey" and she was a lieutenant. Her light green eyes studied his skeptically from within her suit helmet. "It looked very much like you were rendezvousing with the other ship, as though you were planning to make an exchange."

"We were," Spud said. He figured lying would do him no good now. "We weren't given any choice. That is, until you came along and scared them off."

"You weren't given any choice?" Grey's eyes narrowed.

"No," Spud said. "And honestly? It seems more and more like the cargo they wanted us to exchange is something I'd rather not have on my ship, so you can take it. In fact, I recommend you inspect it immediat—"

"Take off your helmet and suits," she ordered.

Spud nodded at Finn and Glossy. As soon as they'd stepped out of their suits, one of the male soldiers grabbed Spud's arms and began to cuff him.

"Hey, is this necessary?" Spud said, eyeing Finn and Glossy as they were grabbed and cuffed too. "We're not resisting you."

"Yes, it's necessary," Grey said bluntly, taking off her own helmet, as one or two strands of blond curls, fell about her face from the bun she wore. "You're a thief."

"No," Spud said. "I'm just a cargo runner who got played."

She smiled. "Of course you are." She pulled a small data-pane from her suit pocket. "Our records show this ship has a crew of six. Is that correct?"

"Yes. The others are on the flight deck with our passenger. I believe it's her cargo you want."

Grey glanced at her data-pane. "Lieutenant Shayla Morrison." She looked back at Spud. "Your girlfriend."

"*Ex*-girlfriend. *Ex* being the emphasis there," Spud replied.

Grey tapped her device then held the screen up to show Spud images of himself and Shayla stumbling along drunk on New Moon Station, faces stuck together. "Ex, you say?"

Spud cringed internally. "I was drunk. She took advantage of me."

Grey smiled again. "Of course she did."

"If you've been watching her all this time, why didn't you bust her at Sailor's Junction when she collected the cargo?"

"*We* haven't been watching her. My ship was simply in the area and told to respond to a situation, to track down your ship and arrest Morrison and her accessories. We'll be thoroughly searching this vessel."

"The cargo is right here—" Spud began to stand, but the soldier behind him thrust the butt of his weapon into his back. Spud groaned and folded forward.

"Chancer," Grey disciplined the soldier.

"He made a move!" Chancer replied.

"He's also cuffed," she said firmly.

Spud pressed his forehead against the floor as he breathed through the pain.

"Spud?" Finn asked, checking on him.

"Help him up," Grey ordered.

Spud pulled himself back up to his knees. "I'm fine," he said, though his voice didn't hold the power it normally did.

"Watch yourself," Chancer said in Spud's ear. "We're not playing around here."

Spud stared at the guy. He was pale-skinned and angry-faced.

"Go help round up the others," Grey ordered the soldier.

Chancer looked at her.

"I gave you an order," she repeated.

Chancer hesitated a moment, then obeyed, kicking past Spud as he did.

Spud watched the soldier leave. "Nice guy."

● ● ●

Spud, along with his crew and Shayla, were gathered in the cargo hold, cuffed and kneeling on the floor, guarded by two of the soldiers named Renton and Shaw, while Chancer, Grey and the two others searched their ship. Renton looked young, maybe nineteen years old at best; he chewed gum and shook his leg with nervous excitement. Spud figured they probably didn't get to see much action out here in The Wastelands, so this arrest would make his day. Shaw looked older, calmer, his eyes moving carefully over each of Spud's crew.

"I can't believe you just served me up on a plate!" Shayla hissed at Spud.

He looked at her. "I can't believe you dragged me into this mess!" he hissed back. "You didn't think they'd search the security footage on the stations or the drone footage on the docks to track where you went? *Wow*, you've really lost your surveillance skills," he said sarcastically, throwing her words from the bar when they'd met, back at her. "That's sloppy, Shayla, even for you."

She scowled back at him. "Fuck you!"

"No, fuck you!" Nikita spat at her. "You've dragged us *all* into this mess, you little bitch!"

"We should throw her outside," Glossy muttered, eyes dark.

Shayla looked away from them. "You might as well. If you don't do it, then Guantano will."

"No, he won't," Spud said, "because you'll be rotting in a navy prison."

"Guantano is everywhere!" Shayla shot back.

Chancer, Grey and the other two soldiers, named Dante and Harper, returned to the cargo hold. Spud took a good look at them. Dante was hairless and muscular. Harper was bearded and tattooed, and though less muscular than Dante, still pretty solid.

"So?" Spud asked. "Find any other illegal items?"

"Only this." Grey held up the syringe and vial of fluid. "In your quarters."

Spud stared at it.

"That's mine," King blurted. "I'm the medical officer. I was chatting to Spud in his room and I must've left them there."

Grey studied the vial, then tucked it in her pocket along with the syringe.

"How did you know the trade was going down?" Shayla asked Grey. "Who tipped you off?"

"A theft was reported." Grey looked at her data-pane. "Then a soldier by the name of Robertson volunteered to help with our enquiries."

"Robertson?" Shayla clenched her teeth. "That *asshole!*"

"Oh," Spud said, "don't like it when someone BETRAYS YOU, Shayla?"

She flicked him a glare and Spud turned back to Grey who was watching them. "Can you please take her with that cargo? I want her off my ship."

"We're taking all of you," Grey said.

"We haven't done anything wrong," Spud said. "We got duped, is all."

"We've checked your crew files. You're all ex-military, most with dubious histories," Grey said. "This woman is your ex-girlfriend. You honestly expect us to believe that you weren't in on this heist?"

"Yes, that's exactly what I'm saying. She paid me to run cargo. At no point did she say, 'Hey Spud, wanna help me rip off the navy and sell to the mob?' Because I assure you I would've said no."

Grey shrugged. "You're under arrest and this ship is impounded until further investigations can be made."

"What!" Glossy exclaimed.

Nikita glared at Spud. "I am going to beat the living shit out of you for this."

He looked at Grey. "Hey, look, you've searched my ship and found nothing else incriminating. Whoever gave you that image of me and Shayla on New Moon Station, would've seen her call me *inside* the bar. I had no idea she was going to be there. She set me up and used me."

"So," Grey said, "you still aided in a felony."

"I didn't know it was a felony until you showed up."

"Which one is your cargo?" Grey looked at Shayla.

Shayla looked down at her knees.

Grey moved over to her. "Which one?" she demanded.

"It's against the wall," Spud said, and motioned with his head to the box behind where Chancer stood.

The soldier turned and walked over to it. "This one?" He slapped his hand down on the lid.

A bang sounded back from within.

Chancer flinched and everyone turned to stare at it.

Spud and Finn exchanged an uneasy glance.

"What the hell's inside?" Chancer asked as Grey stepped closer to it.

"It's classified," Shayla said quickly.

Chancer moved to strike the lid again.

"Don't!" Finn said.

"Why not?" Chancer asked.

"I heard a hissing sound coming from inside earlier. Something was broken. Leaking."

"So?" Chancer said bending his ear closer to it.

"What's inside?" Grey asked Shayla firmly.

"You don't know?" Shayla asked her curiously.

"All I know is that we had to pick up a thief and her stolen cargo. What's in the box?"

"I told you, I don't know," Shayla replied.

"How do you know you've got the right cargo then?" Grey asked her.

"He's right, I hear hissing," Chancer said, standing upright. "What the hell's inside?"

Shayla kept her eyes on the floor.

"Why's it hissing?" Chancer asked again. "What's that mean?"

"Did you rig it with something?" Grey asked.

Shayla looked at the box, then shook her head.

"Where'd it come from?" Grey asked. "What's inside?"

"I told you I don't know," Shayla said.

Chancer moved to Shayla, grabbed a handful of her hair and yanked her head back viciously. "What's inside?" he yelled.

Shayla grunted but said nothing.

"WHAT'S INSIDE?" he shouted, yanking her head again.

"Hey," Spud said, "ease off. She said she didn't know."

"And you believe her?" Chancer said, shoving her away.

"Someone better tell us what's inside that box," Grey said. "*Now!*"

"She said it came from Quadrant Four," Spud said, breaking the silence.

"What's Quadrant Four?" Grey asked.

Spud shrugged and glanced at Finn.

"What's Quadrant Four?" Grey demanded, looking at Finn now.

Finn stared back at her. "Things the navy don't want us to know about."

Chancer charged his stun weapon and stormed over to Finn. "What's inside the box?!"

"Chancer!" Grey barked, as the soldier pressed the gun to Finn's temple.

"What do you know?" Chancer said. "What is that hissing? Is it going to blow?"

"All I know is what I just told you," Finn said through gritted teeth.

"What is it?!" Chancer yelled.

"I told you!" Finn shot back, trying to control the volume of his own voice.

Chancer smacked the weapon across Finn's head, sending him to the floor.

"HEY!" Spud yelled.

"Chancer!" Grey barked again, storming up to him. "Back off."

The soldier turned around to her. "Or you'll what?" He stepped toward her. His larger frame would be intimidating to some, but Grey stepped right up to it.

"I am in command here and you will obey my orders," she said firmly.

Chancer stared her down. Grey stared back, unflinching.

"I will not stand for your bullshit," Grey said firmly. "So. *Back. Off.*"

Chancer stared at her for a moment, then glanced at the other soldiers. They stared back, not appearing to take any sides. Chancer looked back at Grey, then lowered his gun.

"Help him up," Grey ordered. Chancer looked down at Finn, then grabbed his arm and yanked him back to his knees. Spud saw blood dripping down the side of Finn's face.

"You alright?" he asked Finn.

His crewman shook his head as though to clear his vision, then gave Spud a pained nod.

Spud looked at Grey. "Look, we have no idea what's in that cargo, and I assure you the hissing sound bothers us, too."

"What's in Quadrant Four?" Grey asked Finn. "And if it's so classified, how do you know about it?"

Finn looked at her and shrugged. "I'm ex-navy. I was posted there for a time. I'd love to tell you about it, except I'd prefer to live."

"Is the hissing noise a problem?" Grey asked him.

Finn looked at her, blood still dripping down his cheek. "I don't know. Quadrant Four is where they work on prototypes. It could be a weapon about to blow, it could be a biological contaminant leaking out... I don't know."

Grey stared at him for a moment, mind ticking over. "Shit," she said, turning to look at the box. "We can't take it back to our ship. Not if it poses a threat to the rest of our crew."

"So what do we do?" the soldier named Shaw asked, holding his weapon tightly.

Grey exhaled and clicked on her comms. "*Saputra*, this is Lieutenant Grey. I need to speak with the colonel. Get him online."

Silence sat for a moment, while Grey walked back over to the container, speaking in hushed tones.

Spud looked from Finn's bleeding head to the concerned eyes of the rest of his crew: Miguel, Glossy, Nikita, King. He looked at Shayla.

"Shayla, if you know something and you're not telling us..."

She looked back at him, and for the first time he saw worry in her eyes. "I don't know what's in there, Spud. I just had to get it to the *Palomar* pick up point. I swear."

Grey ended her comms and came back to the group. "Alright, we're not leaving until we know what we're dealing with. The colonel's going to find out what he can, but in the meantime, we need to know what that hissing is. Seal the door to the outer bay." Grey motioned for Dante and Renton to do it. They moved over and closed it.

Spud heard the sound of the navy transfer ship unlocking from the other side of the hatch and pull away.

"Where are they going?" Harper, hearing it too, looked at Grey.

"They're pulling back until we know what we're dealing with."

"They're leaving us here?" Renton asked.

"They're just pulling back to safety. We can't risk the transfer chute or our navy vessel."

"What if this thing blows up?" Dante asked, pointing at the box.

Grey looked at him. "Then we all blow up with it." She looked back at the *Benobi* crew. "So this is your last chance. What is in the box?"

No one answered.

"Why is the box hissing?" Grey said more firmly. "Are we at risk? Because none of us are moving until we know what's inside."

"I told you, I don't know," Shayla said, begrudgingly. "I think it's some kind of weapon. That's why Guantano wanted it. But I don't know what it is."

"Could it be a bomb?" Grey asked.

Shayla shrugged.

"You said it was fragile," Spud said to Shayla.

"They said to keep it steady, not shake it about. They said to keep things chilled."

"Chilled?" Grey asked. "Is it a chemical weapon? Something biological?"

"It could be a coolant hose that's gone inside," Harper said, scratching his beard nervously. "Shaw can fix that."

Shaw nodded, stepping toward the box. "Yeah. Piece of cake."

"Wait!" Grey said. "We don't know if that's what it is yet."

"But if it is," Glossy spoke up. "If there is a malfunction with the coolant, what does it mean if the thing inside warms up and overheats?"

"If it's biological," Miguel offered, "that could be a problem. What if it's a virus?"

Grey looked at Spud. "You're running cargo. You must have some equipment that can scan the thing."

Spud looked back at her. "The cargo is scanned on the docks before we load it."

"And did you scan this?"

Spud looked at his ex. "Shayla did."

A look of guilt slid over her face.

"Shayla?" he prodded.

"It was classified, Spud," she said. "You don't ask questions and you certainly don't scan the thing and leave a record."

"How did you get it past security?" Grey asked.

"You can buy anyone for the right price," Shayla said quietly.

Grey's face hardened. "There's nothing here on this ship that will help us look inside that thing without opening it?" she asked Spud.

"I could try a body sensor," King offered. "It's small and meant for humans but depending on what that box is made out of, I *might* be able to read through it. That will at least tell us if it's biological or not."

"Do it," Grey ordered. "Shaw, Chancer, go with him."

Shaw nodded and Chancer yanked King to his feet and marched him out of the cargo hold.

CHAPTER SEVEN

Spud watched as Grey paced, talking in hushed tones into her comms. When she finished, she moved over to stand in front of Finn.

"What's Exosis?"

"Exosis?" Finn furrowed a brow at her.

"That's the company the box originated from."

"I haven't heard of them," Finn said. "Where are they based?"

"Quadrant Four."

"Yeah, but where in Quadrant Four? There're four different sectors and I only worked in one of them."

"Look," Spud said to Grey, "if that thing is possibly a bomb or a contagion, how about you uncuff us so we stand a chance if things turn to shit?"

Grey looked at him. "No."

"So you're just going to let us die?"

"If things turn to shit, and it's not *you* causing the shit, then I'll uncuff you," Grey said. "Until then, you stay cuffed."

Chancer and Shaw returned then with King. Grey motioned them toward the box. "Do what you can," she ordered.

"My hands?" King said. Grey studied him a moment, then gave the nod to uncuff him.

Chancer did so, then shoved his stunner in King's back. "Slow, careful movements."

King held his hands out in a peaceful gesture and gave a nod, and they watched as he took the small hand-held device and began to run it over the side of the box. It wasn't long, though, before he stopped and sighed.

"I don't know what this box is made of," he said, "but I can't scan through it. The walls must be impenetrable. I don't think this box is designed to be scanned."

"So what do we do?" Chancer asked, shaking his leg. "We could be sitting on a ticking bomb here."

Grey stepped closer. "How does it open?"

"Is that a good idea?" Spud asked quickly.

"I don't see any latches or locks, just lights," she said, stepping closer to the box. "So there must be a console." She began running her fingers over every inch of the box, seeking a button or something. "If there's a console, maybe we can access information that way."

"There's a data port on the edge of the lid," Glossy said, watching carefully from where she knelt.

Grey looked at her.

Glossy shrugged back. "I was curious. It's a top-line casing. Expensive stuff. It can only be accessed by connecting it to a console."

Grey ran her hand along the lid until her fingers found a small hole. She looked back at Glossy. "Is this it? Bring her here?"

Renton grabbed Glossy and brought her over to Grey. She eyed the port.

"Yeah, that's it. You'll need to connect a data console to access it."

"Did you do this already?" Grey asked her.

Glossy shook her head. "No. Cap's orders."

Grey pulled out her data-pane. "Will this do?"

Glossy nodded. "But you'll need a cable. I'll have one at my worktable. Over there, by the door," she motioned.

"Turn around," Grey ordered, and when Glossy did, Grey uncuffed the Benobi's engineer. "Shaw, take her to get the cable and bring her back here."

Spud watched as Glossy was led over to her table. He glanced back at King and noticed his hands were still uncuffed. He felt a little better knowing at least some of his crew had their hands free. He'd be happier if there were a few more, though.

"Hey, lieutenant," he said to Grey. "You mind if we get something to eat?" He tried to glance at his data-band to see the time. "It's almost breakfast time anyway. I'm starving."

Grey considered him as Glossy came back with the cable.

"You seem to know what you're doing," Grey said to Glossy, handing over her data-pane. "See if you can connect to that box and find out what's inside."

Glossy gave a nod, took the pane and plugged it in. Grey caught her arm. "Careful now. No big moves without my authorization," she said, eyeing the data-pane now in Glossy's hands.

Glossy nodded and Grey looked back at Spud.

"Food?" he asked again.

"This could take a while." Glossy backed him up.

"Renton, Dante," Grey said to the other two soldiers, "grab some food from the mess."

Miguel straightened. "Hey! It's my mess. Take me. You won't know where anything is," he gruffed.

"He's protective of the mess," Spud said, "but he makes damn tasty food. You should try some."

Grey stared at Spud, then gave a motion for them to take Miguel.

Spud smiled inwardly as an uncuffed Miguel left with the two men. He looked back at Nikita, Finn and Shayla still cuffed beside him, then turned his eyes warily back to the box.

● ● ●

The silence sat as Glossy tried to access the box's data. Grey had not allowed them to be uncuffed while they'd eaten and had instead made King and Miguel feed them, but at least Spud's belly was content, now. Although he would kill for a coffee. Still, he felt a little better that Grey had allowed King to dress Finn's head wound.

Sitting cross-legged on the floor now, Spud noticed Grey analyzing him, her mind turning something over. He stared back, curious.

"Something wrong?" he asked her.

"You don't look like the senator at all," she said.

Spud straightened.

"The senator?" Finn asked.

Grey's eyes kindled with curiosity as they danced around the *Benobi* crew then back to Spud. "They don't know Senator Whitlam is your father?"

Spud exhaled heavily, shoulders slumping. "They do now."

"You didn't tell them?" Shayla smiled, feigning surprise. "I thought you didn't lie, Spud."

"I didn't *lie*," he said. "I just... didn't tell them."

"Senator Whitlam's your father?" King asked, surprised.

"Senator Whitlam?!" Renton echoed. "That means Tiberius Whitlam is your brother."

"Tiberius?" Dante asked. "*The* Tiberius? As in Major Timothy 'Tiberius' Whitlam?"

"No way this piece of shit is Tiberius' brother!" Chancer scoffed.

Spud looked back at Grey. "And you wonder why I kept it quiet," he said flatly. "There's no living up to my hero big brother, or my military-loving father."

"Your brother is a *goddamn hero*!" Chancer said, kicking him. "And your father is a good man. He supports us! Makes sure we're taken care of!"

"That he does."

"You don't share their way of thinking?" Grey asked, eyes still sparkling with curiosity.

"I share DNA with them. That's all. I can't help that."

"You ought to be ashamed, man!" Dante said. "Talking about them like that."

"Yeah, yeah," Spud sighed.

"But you started out in the navy?" Grey said.

"I did," Spud gave a nod. "I wasn't really given a choice in the matter. But," he shrugged, "turns out, I'm a lover not a fighter."

"That why you're using your mother's name, Compton?" Grey asked.

"For someone who's just been pulled in on this mission, you sure seem to know a lot about me," his eyes sparkled curiously back at hers.

"I do," she said. "Unlike you, I research a job when it's given to me. I don't take it on blind faith."

"Blind *lust* you mean," Nikita muttered.

Spud shot his pilot an "unfair" look.

"Oh, come on, Spud," Nikita said. "You were pussy-whipped and now we're stuck in this shit. Admit that at least!"

The soldiers laughed at him.

Shayla grinned and peacocked. "What can I say, I'm hard to resist."

"I've seen a lot better." Grey shut her down coldly.

Spud shot Shayla a satisfied smile.

"I'm in!" Glossy announced.

Spud's spine straightened and Grey's head whipped around to the engineer.

"What does it say?" Grey leaned over Glossy's shoulder to view the screen.

"I don't know yet," she replied. "I'm not familiar with this system."

They watched silently as Glossy tapped at the pane, various screens flicking over on the display, and text scrolling here and there.

"Panthera-X03..." Glossy mused aloud.

"What's that?" Grey asked.

"It's the product name," Glossy said. "That's the contents. One Panthera-X03."

"Anyone heard of that before?" Grey asked, glancing around.

"If it's from Quadrant Four, no one will have heard of it," Finn said.

Grey studied him. "You've never heard of a company or anything similar to this name," she glanced back at the screen, "Panthera?"

"Panthera means cat," Miguel said. "It's the name of the family of cats that lions and jaguars belong to."

Grey turned her stare to him.

Miguel shrugged. "I'm a cat lover."

"Yeah, but is it a cat inside," Shaw said, "or is that just a cool name for a new laser weapon or bomb?"

Grey turned back to Glossy. "Keep searching."

Glossy did as ordered, tapping away at the screen, until a beep sounded. She tapped her finger again and another beep sounded. "It requires a code for me to access any further information."

Grey looked back at Finn. "Come here."

Renton pulled Finn to his feet and brought him to her.

"Does any of this other jargon mean anything to you?" She held the pane out to him. His eyes darted over the screen and he shook his head. Grey brought up the next screen and he continued, then she tapped over to the next screen.

"Wait," Finn said, "go back to the last screen." She did, and Finn took a moment to reread the data. "There," he said motioning toward the top of the screen with his bandaged head. "Quadrant Four, Sector 4." He looked at Grey. "It's biological."

"How can you be sure?"

"Because that's what Sector 4 did. They handled all the biological stuff. I worked a different sector, so that's as much as I can tell you. But it's safe to say that this isn't an explosive."

"But it could be some kind of virus bomb."

Finn shrugged. "Maybe. But airborne viruses are a threat to everyone, not just our enemies. The navy prefer the kind of weapons with a more controlled output."

"So what the hell's inside then?" Chancer asked.

Grey looked back at the box, then turned away, clicking on her comms again. This time, she left the cargo hold, stepping out into the *Benobi's* corridor.

"Maybe we should just open it?" Renton suggested.

"Oh, that's a great idea," Spud said sarcastically, eyeing him. "We have absolutely no idea what's inside this mystery box from the highly classified Quadrant Four, but let's just open it anyway."

"We can't open the box," Shayla spoke up. They all turned to look at her. "I was told to keep the box still and steady, to keep things chilled, and to *never* open the box."

"Maybe they didn't want you seeing what was inside," Chancer said. "Then you'd know you could sell it for five times what they were offering you."

Shayla stared at him, her mind ticking over.

Grey reappeared.

"What'd the colonel say?" Shaw asked.

"He's looking into things. He's been trying to find out what it is, but the folks at Exosis aren't being cooperative. He's going to speak with Admiral Eames."

"Admiral Eames?" King said. "Holy shit. It's gone right to the top?"

Grey nodded.

"Sounds like we're at a stalemate," Spud said. "The left hand of the navy isn't talking to the right hand."

Grey looked at him but didn't respond.

Chancer stepped up to the box again, and bent over it, placing his ear against the lid. The silence sat as everyone watched him.

"I don't hear the hissing anymore," he said. "I don't hear anything."

"The hissing's stopped?" Grey asked, but she was cut off when Chancer raised his hand to hush her.

"Wait," he said, listening intently. "I think I just heard... I think it's a..." He stood up and looked at them, confused. "It sounds like a kitten."

"A kitten!" Nikita furrowed her brow.

"This isn't the time for jokes, Chancer!" Grey scolded him.

"I'm not! Listen!"

Grey eyed Chancer, saw he was serious, then motioned for Shaw to listen. The soldier bent down and pressed his ear against the lid. They watched and waited. Finally he heard something, pulled back, then stared down at the lid. "He's right. It's a damn kitten."

"A kitten?" Glossy frowned.

"Panthera..." Miguel mused aloud.

"You stole a kitten for the mob?" Spud asked Shayla.

"The hissing must've been an oxygen leak," Renton said. "The thing's probably suffocating and crying for help or something."

"That *thing* came from Quadrant Four," Finn warned.

King nodded. "It may be a kitten but it could be infected with a virus."

"Tell the admiral it's just a kitten and let's get back on the ship and on our way," Chancer said.

Grey moved up to the box and placed her ear against the lid. She listened for a moment, then stood again. "Why the hell would everyone go to this much trouble over a kitten?" She looked back at King. "It has to be infected with something or carrying some kind of classified intel."

"It doesn't matter," Chancer said. "It's a kitten. It's no threat. Let's load it and go."

Grey suddenly turned and pressed her earpiece. "Yes, sir?" She listened for a moment, then turned her eyes back to the box. "Yes, sir. We've heard a... what appears to be a... *kitten*... inside, sir. Yes, sir. A kitten. I heard it myself. It's alive, but we're still not sure what the hissing sound was. It's stopped now, but there could've been a malfunction with the box, maybe the oxygen supply. If this kitten is so precious to Exosis, what do they want us to do about it?" Grey began to pace, listening. "Is there any threat of an airborne contagion, sir? What about skin contact? We're not equipped to handle anything like that, unless we resupply from the *Saputra*." Grey continued to pace. "Are you sure, sir?" Her eyes scanned the soldiers, then turned back to the box. "I'd prefer that, sir. Thank you." She ended the comms and looked back at her team. "Our crew on the *Saputra* will send us some biosuits and a tranquilizer gun. They want us to open the box, ensure the kitten has enough oxygen and tranq it. Exosis want the contents back alive."

"Tell Exosis to come and sort it out themselves," Spud said.

"There's no time," Grey said.

"What about the rest of us?" King asked. "Are you supplying enough suits for all of us?"

"No. Just us." She looked at Glossy. "And you."

"Me?" Glossy asked.

"If there's a problem with the O^2 system, Shaw might need your help. You can fix it, yes? You're the engineer, right?"

"Ah," Glossy threw Spud a look. "I can try."

"You're putting us at risk if you expose us to what's inside," King said.

"It's a kitten," Chancer said derogatorily.

"From Quadrant Four," Spud said, then turned to Grey. "I can't allow you to put my crew's lives at risk."

"They won't be. We'll move you out of the cargo hold while we do it."

"What about the air systems?" King asked.

"I've been assured the Panthera-X03 is not infected with any airborne contagions. The suits are to protect us from any scratches. There *is* a risk of infection if the claws make contact."

"Claws?" Nikita asked.

"What'd they infect it with?" King asked.

"I'm not sure we want to know," Finn said, exchanging a look with him.

"It's a kitten," Chancer said again, looking down his nose at them as though they were cowards. "We open it, tranq the fucker and get on our way."

"That's a mighty big box for a kitten, don't you think?" Spud said with an equal amount of derision.

"Maybe it's a lot of kittens?" Nikita said.

Spud looked at Grey. "I don't like this."

"We don't have any choice," she said. "We need to return the cargo to Exosis but we can't move it until we know the goods inside are okay and that there's no threat to the crew on my vessel."

"But it's okay for *my* crew to be at threat?"

"You perhaps should've thought of that before you took the cargo on in the first place."

"I didn't know!"

"How do you plan to open the box?" Glossy asked, shifting the conversation. "Did they give you the access codes?"

Grey nodded, studying the data-pane in her hands. "I have full access now."

"Glossy? You sure about this?" Spud asked her, concerned.

Glossy studied the soldiers, then looked back at Spud, nodded and smiled. "I'm happy to help the navy, Spud," she said, working hard to avoid jail time. "Let's just fix this and get on our way."

Grey turned to her team. "Clear the cargo hold and prepare for the suit delivery."

CHAPTER EIGHT

Spud stood, hands still cuffed behind his back, in the corridor at the ship's inner door to the cargo hold. Guarded by Shaw and Dante, his crew, with the exception of Glossy, stood with him. Spud's face was close to the door's observation window, watching carefully as Grey's team, inside the cargo hold and dressed in biosuits, prepared to open the box.

"I got a bad feeling about this," Nikita said, close by his side.

"Me, too," Spud said, subconsciously pulling on his cuffs.

"That's not a kitten inside," Finn said. "Not if it came from Quadrant Four. It might look and sound like a kitten, but it won't be."

"Panthera-X03 does not sound like a kitten's name," Miguel said gravely.

"The risk is infection from the claws, right?" King asked. "Should I prep the med bay?"

"No one's going anywhere," Shaw said, hands wrapped tightly around his weapon.

"Could you remove my cuffs, please?" Spud asked. "I'm the captain of this ship, and if shit goes down, I need to respond."

"You won't need to respond. That's what we're here for," Dante said.

"Yeah?" Spud said, eyeing him. Though Dante was well-built, he looked only 24 or 25 years old. "Well, if things go bad, no offence, I'd prefer to rely on my own team than yours for my defense."

"Shut up," Shaw said. "It's a goddamn kitten with bacteria in its claws. Relax."

"Do you at least have the keys to our cuffs?" Nikita asked.

Shaw shook his head. "Grey and Chancer have them."

Spud turned back to the window. "And they're inside. Great."

Spud watched as Grey, Chancer, Harper and Renton, dressed in biosuits, began to open the box. Glossy was ordered to stand well back until called upon. That was something at least, Spud thought. Grey wasn't being reckless with his crew.

Grey stood by the console, working her data-pane, while Chancer, Renton and Harper stood with their weapons raised and spread around the container, which was placed in the middle of the clear floor space. Harper held the tranq gun.

"The code worked," Grey said, her voice pouring through the comms speaker in the corridor. "We're in."

They watched as a high-pitched alarm sounded and red lights along the top of the box began to flash.

To Spud, they looked like warning lights.

"The lid's unlocked," Grey said. "Renton, Harper, Chancer, get ready."

The silence hung thickly in the corridor as Grey tapped her console once more. Spud noted the top of the box reached Grey's upper chest height. With a whir of hydraulics, the lid on the box began to retract, and a smoky substance wafted over the edges and disappeared into the air.

"What is that?" Miguel asked.

"Remnants of the cooling system?" King said.

"Or something else," Nikita said, eyes fixed on the box.

When the box was partway open, Grey and Chancer paused, studying the contents.

"What is that?" Grey asked motioning to something.

"Shredded... paper?" Chancer asked.

The lid was now fully retracted, and they swiftly pointed their weapons inside.

"What's inside?" Spud asked, but they, of course, couldn't hear him.

Both Grey and Chancer peered carefully into the box, the red lights along the top of it reflecting off their helmet faceplates. Chancer used the barrel of his weapon to move something aside. He then lifted his weapon and they saw something hanging off the end. It was strips of something that were a pinky-beige in color. *The shredded paper?*

"What is it?" Grey asked.

"It looks like," Chancer pulled the long, ragged strip off the end of his weapon and studied it. "I think it's... skin."

"Skin?" King said, two down from Spud along the window. "That's a lot of skin for a kitten."

"Where's the fur?" Nikita asked.

"Did it shed this?" Grey asked quickly, darting her eyes between the skin and the box as she tightened the grip on her weapon. "Or did it eat whatever this used to be?"

Spud looked at Shaw. "Tell them to be careful!"

"They know what they're doing!" he said, watching his team intently.

The sound of a kitten's *meow* caught their attention. Spud looked at the box. Chancer shook the sheet of skin to the floor and held his weapon back in place.

The kitten meowed again.

Grey suddenly stepped backward, her weapon held tighter. "Something moved!"

"Yeah, it's in there," Chancer said. "It's hiding beneath all this skin."

"It's probably just frightened," Renton said.

"How big is it?" Harper asked. "Do we even need the tranq?"

"It's hiding," Chancer said, moving his head back and forth trying to get a better look.

"We need to see if anything needs fixing," Grey said. "Let's get this done. Pull the skin back, tranq the animal, and let's check the box."

Chancer nodded and made clear eye contact with Harper, then Renton, and then Grey. "Keep me covered now," he said, then lowered his weapon and swung it over his shoulder. He looked in the box. "Here, kitty, kitty…"

Spud's heart kicked up a notch. He saw Glossy glance over to him. He gave her a smile of assurance. She smiled back like she needed it, then returned her attention to the box.

Chancer began to slowly pull more sheets of skin out of the box, dumping them on the floor. "Here kitt—"

Another *meow* sounded, but this was one different.

It was deeper.

Adult.

"What the hell was that?" Grey demanded.

Chancer paused, one hand gripping the strap of his weapon, ready to deploy. "There must be more than one in here." He reached forward with this free hand and pulled back another, larger, sheet of shed skin, then glanced in the box. "Oh, SHIT!"

Chancer threw himself backward as something large and pink leaped out of the box with a loud snarl.

The hairless, muscled lump of meat hit Chancer at speed, knocking him to the floor with a sickening thud. With its jaws clamped around the man's throat, it began shaking him like a rag doll.

"Fuck!" Harper yelled in surprise, before trying to take aim with the tranq gun.

The cargo hold was suddenly an erratic light show as Renton fired his weapon—switched to laser fire—at the moving creature, while Grey screamed for both of them not to hit Chancer. Renton hit the creature on its rump, and it gave a wounded whine before suddenly fleeing into a dark gap between a pile of crates in the corner of the cargo hold.

Spud darted his eyes back to Chancer who lay gargling his last breaths, his biosuit and throat torn open, and a river of blood running out onto the floor.

"Fuck!" Spud said. "Uncuff me! Open the door! GLOSSY!"

Glossy, alarmed, gravitated backward to the door, as the three remaining soldiers crowded their fallen comrade, weapons raised in the direction where the animal disappeared.

"What the hell *was* that?" Nikita panted in horror.

"It looked like a skinned chicken!" King said.

"That was a big goddamned chicken!" Finn said.

"No," Miguel shook his head. "Panthera. More like a jaguar. A big hairless jaguar."

"Uncuff us!" Spud shouted.

"Shut up!" Shaw yelled, peering through the window at his team.

"Uncuff us!"

"Shut up!" Dante drove the butt of his weapon into Spud's side, dropping him to his knees with a groan.

"Stop!" King yelled, leaning over Spud in protection. "Stop it!"

"SHUT UP!" Shaw yelled. "SHUT THE FUCK UP OR I'LL SHOOT."

"Alright!" Finn said. "Alright! Just calm down!"

"Glossy!" Nikita called. "Open the door. Get out of there!"

"Nobody moves," Dante yelled. "Grey's orders!"

"That was *before* that thing burst out!" Nikita said.

Dante raised his weapon and pressed the barrel to her forehead. "I said *no*."

"Okay, okay!" King said calmly hands up in surrender. "Everyone just calm down."

"Where the hell did it go!" they heard Grey's strained voice say.

Spud got himself on his feet with another groan and peered in the window. All he could hear was their panting breaths over the comms. Renton stood waving his weapon about nervously, Harper knelt with his hand pressed against Chancer's throat, his head bowed in grief, while Grey stood rigid. Her eyes were fixed on the spot the Panthera had fled to.

"Is he alive?" she asked Harper, not taking her eyes off the darkened corner of the cargo hold.

"He's gone," Harper said. "He's fucking dead."

"You want one of us in there?" Shaw spoke into his comms.

"No," Grey said firmly. "Glossy?"

"Yeah?"

"Get out into the corridor until we take this thing down."

Glossy nodded and continued to move backward. "I'm not going to argue with that."

"If you uncuff me," Spud said calmly to Shaw, "I can help you get that thing."

They heard another *meow* and all looked back through the window.

"It sounds like a damn kitten," Miguel said, eyes narrowed. "How does it sound like that?"

"They would've engineered it that way," Finn said, sweat beading across his brow. "To lure its prey. It doesn't sound like a threat. It's the perfect trap."

Suddenly a stack of boxes shifted and swayed.

"It's on the move!" Grey said. "It's pushing its way between the crates."

"Let's just shoot the damn thing!" Renton yelled. He began firing at every box that moved.

"No!" Grey yelled, but the soldier ignored her. Laser fire lit up the room. "Renton, stop! CEASE FIRE!"

"He's going to set the cargo alight!" Spud breathed in horror.

They watched as some of the wooden crates and stacks of cardboard boxes that he hit with the laser began to smoke and then flame.

"Shit!" Grey hissed, searching the ceiling for something. *The fire systems?*

Renton lowered his weapon, realizing his error. Glossy saw the growing flames and moved away from the door, sprinting toward a small fire extinguisher attached to the wall near the outer bay door.

"Glossy!" Spud called, but it was useless. She couldn't hear them inside the hold. Glossy pulled the latch, moved carefully toward the cargo and began to deploy the extinguisher at the flames.

The Panthera sounded again, but it wasn't a kitten's meow, it was a deeper snarl. A pissed-off growl.

"It doesn't like the smoke," King said. "Or maybe the extinguisher?"

More boxes and crates moved, on the right-hand side of the hold, near the door to the outer bay, which wasn't far from the door to the rest of the ship where Spud stood now. The soldiers in the cargo bay still stood toward the far left-hand corner where it had first disappeared.

"It's moving around them," Spud said. "If it gets around them, it's going to block them off from all their exits." He looked at Shaw. "Tell Grey to drive it back!"

Shaw looked nervously through the window.

"Tell them!" Spud yelled.

"Grey—" Shaw began, but stopped suddenly as the *Benobi*'s fire system suddenly kicked in and water began to rain down upon them.

"Shit!" Grey said, looking about and wiping the splattered visor of her biosuit. "Shit!" She tried to wipe down her gun, but it was no use. "Laser and stunner fire off!" she called. "We'll fry in this water!"

"Fuck!" Renton yelled, smacking himself in the head for his stupidity.

"Burners on!" Grey yelled, igniting her weapon's flamethrower. "Watch the cargo!"

The boxes jostled as the creature moved again, closer to the sealed door of the outer bay.

"It's a cat," Miguel said. "It can hear us. It can hear another food source."

"Jesus, it's going to cut us off!" Grey said, realizing. "Push it back, push it back!" She stormed forward to place herself between the moving boxes near the outer bay door and the door into the corridor, projecting a flame of orange fire toward it, but out of range of the cargo. The flame coughed and spluttered under the water sprinkling down from the fire systems. "Renton! Harper! Help me drive it back. Glossy, get behind us!"

Renton moved up beside her. "Let's burn this fucker!"

"Come on, you piece of shit!" Harper yelled, throwing flame, but it flickered and limped under the water that continued to sprinkle down on them.

"Hold your fire until you see it!" Grey barked. "Stay back from the cargo!"

Silence sat as they each swung their weapons back and forth searching for the creature, for any sign on movement. Renton eventually huffed and tore off his biosuit helmet.

"Can't see with that damn thing on!" he said, quickly pulling his whole suit off.

Harper and Grey seemed to agree and did the same, one by one, while the other two covered them.

A sudden movement caught their attention. Chancer's dead body swiftly vanished into the darkened gap between the boxes. They swung their weapons back to the spot, only to see the smear of blood that remained, now being washed away by the spray from above.

Then they heard crunching, tearing sounds.

"It's eating him..." Renton said, mouth agape. "It's fucking eating him! CHANCER!" The soldier began to storm toward the gap in the cargo.

"Renton!" Grey yelled. "Hold! Chill out!"

Harper's face screwed in repulsion at the sound. "Oh, man..."

"How long has it been in the box?" Miguel wondered aloud. "It's probably hungry."

"And that shed skin means it's had a growth spurt," Finn added, exchanging a concerned look with Spud. "I'd say it's *very* hungry."

"It's smart," Grey's voice sounded over the speakers, as she nodded to herself. "This thing is smart. It led us away so it could get to the body."

"FUCK!" Renton yelled throwing flame at the gap in the boxes.

"RENTON! CHILL!" Grey yelled again. "Calm the fuck down, *now*, or I'll kill you myself!"

"It's fucking eating him!" he yelled back at her. "We can't just stand here!"

"He's dead, alright! He's dead! We can't save him!"

The sprinklers suddenly stopped. They glanced above, then shook off the last of the water that covered them.

"We need to draw it out," Grey said, clothes sticking to her. "We need to draw it out in the open, then we tranq it."

"I say we fucking burn it!" Harper said.

"We try the tranq first," Grey said. "If it comes at you, then you do what you need to."

"How do we draw it out?" Renton asked.

"Bait," she swallowed. "I'll do it."

"You sure?" Harper asked.

"I'm in charge," she said, stepping forward. "I'll do it. You just be ready to shoot. Flank me."

Spud watched as Grey headed toward the watered-down blood smears on the ground in front of the darkened gap. She moved carefully in a steady step-slide progression on the wet floor. Harper and Renton moved around to her sides, ready to get a clear shot if it presented itself.

"Come on," Grey said quietly. Whether it was to the Panthera or to muster her own courage, Spud didn't know. He pulled on his cuffs again, anxious as hell to be able to use his arms again. He glanced about and saw Shayla standing down the corridor a little. Her face looked pale. She didn't appear to want to know what was going on inside the cargo hold. Spud's face hardened at her cowardice, then he turned his eyes back to Grey.

The soldier reached the blood smear and crouched a little, trying to see inside the darkened gap between the boxes.

The snarl sounded again.

Then Chancer's leg came rolling out of the gap.

"Jesus!" Grey said, stepping backward.

Things fell silent as the moments ticked by.

Suddenly the creature growled again, and rammed into a stack of crates, toppling them toward Harper. He flung his hands up to protect himself, as the beast leaped out at Grey.

She swiftly ducked aside, the creature missed, skidded a little on the slippery floor, then leaped straight at Renton who'd stepped toward it, taking aim. He managed to fire one lick of flame, making the creature whine, then growl, before its mouth clamped onto his arm. Renton screamed as the beast yanked hard, shaking its head side to side. Grey moved quickly toward him, slipped once on the wet floor, then recovered, pulled her weapon up and flamed the creature's ass.

With a pained whine and smoke wafting off its rear from both burns, it gave a final tug on its prey, then scuttled among the boxes again, taking Renton's arm with it.

"Fuck!" Grey yelled, running to a screaming Renton, whose shoulder now spurted blood. She grabbed his remaining arm and hauled him back toward the door. Harper had managed to throw the crates off his body and now moved across the slippery floor toward Grey, as the beast sped out again. It moved so fast, Spud barely saw it. Harper turned just as it leaped onto his back and tackled him to the ground.

"Open the door!" Glossy suddenly banged on the window in a panic, making the group in the corridor jump in fright. "Open the door!"

Shaw stepped back unsure what to do.

"Open the goddamn door!" Spud yelled.

"Open it!" Nikita screamed.

"What do we do?" Dante called to Shaw.

Spud looked back to see the creature dragging a fighting Harper back toward the boxes.

"No!" Grey yelled, dropping Renton and running forward again throwing flame at the creature and forcing it back from her soldier.

"Open the GODDAMN DOOR OR THEY'RE ALL GOING TO DIE!" Spud yelled.

"Shit!" Shaw said, hitting the door's release. It slid back and Glossy lunged out of the cargo hold, putting her back against the corridor wall, panting in terror.

"Grey!" Shaw called as he and Dante took up position on either side of the door. Grey threw flame toward the creature again and it darted back inside the darkened hole.

"Uncuff me!" Spud said. "Someone uncuff me!" He looked into the hold to see Chancer's mangled leg laying on the floor, then glanced over to Grey. She was now hauling Harper toward the door and shooting flame toward the creature, which had darted out again, and was now scuttling back to the darkness of the cargo gaps.

"Don't just stand there. Help her!" Spud barked at their guards.

"I got it!" Dante swooped inside the cargo hold and ran toward her. "You shoot the thing if it comes," he said to her, then lowered his weapon, grabbed Harper's bloodied belt and heaved. The thing came racing out, but Grey threw more flame at it. It reared back, hissing, then began to prowl back and forth out of reach of the flame, eyeing up its prey, trying to find a way past.

Seeing it clearly now, Spud could tell that it was a large cat, akin to a jaguar, but bigger—much bigger— and hairless; its skin was a soft pink in color, the muscles beneath powerful and flexing with every movement it made. But what disturbed him the most is that it didn't seem to have eyes. At least, the eyes seemed to sit *beneath* the pink skin like dark oval patches. It reminded him, grossly, of what a kitten fetus looked like. Just bigger and deadlier.

"My arm," Renton screamed. "Don't leave my arm!" Grey approached and grabbed him, but he fought her. "Don't leave my fucking arm!" He pushed her away and she grabbed him again, but he flailed in panic. "My arm!"

In the struggle, amidst the wet floor and the blood pouring from Renton's severed arm, Grey slipped and fell. And the Panthera saw its opening.

In a flash, the thing leaped at them. Dante dropped Harper again and raised his weapon. They heard Renton scream when the Panthera latched onto his leg and ripped him from Grey's slippery grip. She skidded again in the blood and water. The Panthera tore at Renton's throat, then looked up at her, chunks of flesh and blood falling from its mouth.

A tongue of flame from Dante's weapon forced the creature back for a moment, before it gave that kittenish *meow* and lunged again. Grey pulled her weapon up.

"Down, Grey!" Shaw yelled running toward her.

She threw herself backward, weapon held over her throat in protection, as both Shaw and Dante blasted flames at the lunging creature. The thing shrieked and scuttled out of reach, and when they killed the flame they weren't sure what they were seeing.

"Where'd it go?" King asked.

"What is that?" Nikita said.

Spud blinked his eyes, unsure of what he was witnessing. The thing, the creature, looked like a mirage. They could vaguely discern its outline, but it had otherwise disappeared—as though they could see right through it—the only giveaway were the dark patches toward its rear where it had been burned.

"It's invisible!" Glossy gasped.

"No, it's camouflage." Finn swallowed. "That's why it's hairless. What the fuck have they created?"

Spud realized now that the beast hadn't necessarily been moving so fast they couldn't see it, it had instead been flashing in and out of its invisible camouflage.

Their momentary pause in shock was all the Panthera needed to regroup. In a flash it leaped at Dante, its nearest threat.

"Jesus! No!" Grey yelled, as the mirage-creature tackled Dante to the ground and a spray of flame arced in the air from his weapon.

Shaw raced for Grey. He grabbed her, hauled her to her feet, then tried to take aim at the creature. Grey raised her weapon too.

They saw a spray of blood and knew the creature had bested Dante.

"Fall back!" she yelled at Shaw. "Fall back!"

"King!" Spud called urgently. "Get ready to close the door!"

"On it!" he yelled, scooting over to the controls.

Grey moved backward toward them, throwing bursts of flame. Shaw did too.

"Come on!" Nikita yelled at them.

Grey turned and ran at them, bursting through the doorway. Shaw threw one last blast, then did the same.

"Hurry!" Glossy screamed at him as the miraged-Panthera crouched, ready to pounce. Shaw pumped his arms hard, running for his life.

"Close the door now!" Spud yelled, and King slammed the button. The door began to close over. Shaw's eyes went wide, then he twisted his body to the side and just skidded through before it closed. He slammed into Finn, who slammed into the wall, as the Panthera slammed against the closed door. The impact was loud and they all flinched against the opposite wall, watching as the camouflaged thing swiped its large bloodied claws against the glass, cracking it, trying to get inside.

"Jesus!" Spud breathed, wide-eyed.

The attack soon stopped and they stared at the cracked, bloodied glass, waiting to see if it had really gone. Grey, panting heavily, hair wet and body covered in blood, raised her weapon and stepped closer to the window. She looked carefully down one side, then the other, before spotting something. She exhaled in sorrow and raised her hand to her mouth. The others crowded around her and saw the Panthera finishing off Renton.

"Harper's still alive," Shaw said in horror.

They looked to see Harper laying on his stomach, his back torn open, but his arms flailing, trying to move himself along the floor.

"He won't be for long," Grey said quietly, as tears filled her eyes.

"We can't just leave him!" Shaw said.

"You wanna go back in there?" Grey said firmly. "He's gone, Shaw. There's nothing we can do for him. Not without losing more lives."

"Even if you could bring him out," King said, his voice distant, "he won't survive those injuries..."

Silence filled the corridor, as they watched the Panthera effortlessly drag Renton's body over to the darkened gap in the crates, then slink back to Harper, finish him off and drag both his and Dante's bodies to the gap as well. All the while in its mirage-like state.

"How the hell can we fight that thing if it can camouflage itself?" Finn said.

Spud looked at Grey. "Will you uncuff me now?"

She looked back at him, her eyes dazed, blood smeared across her cheek and over her clothes, then nodded. "Turn around."

CHAPTER NINE

Spud relished the feeling of his hands free, rubbing his wrists as he looked around. The rest of his team were also uncuffed. Shayla remained down the corridor a little, on her own.

"Is anyone hurt?" King asked, then looked at Grey. "Did it scratch you?"

She shook her head, still looking through the window. "It's not my blood."

"What the hell do we do now?" Nikita asked.

"We need to call in backup," Grey said, then suddenly patted her pockets and spun around to look back into the cargo hold. "The data-pane's inside. And wet." She looked back at Spud. "I need to access to your flight deck comms."

Spud nodded and went to move, but Miguel caught his arm.

"Wait," Miguel said, staring into the cargo hold. "What the hell is it doing?"

They turned back to look through the glass pane and saw the Panthera climbing up the stacks of crates. It seemed to sense their movement, glanced in their direction, then up toward the roof. Spud's eyes followed its line of sight and saw an air shaft vent.

"It's not..." Glossy spoke his thoughts. "It can't... Can it?"

They watched, astounded, as the Panthera-X03 climbed to the top of the stack, then crouched and leaped up at the vent covering. With a swipe of its powerful paw, the vent cover came away and fell down. The Panthera-X03 fell down with it, before righting itself and climbing back up the stack. It crouched, eyeing the hole in the ceiling of the cargo hold.

"No, no, no, no..." Nikita breathed.

They watched in horror as the Panthera leaped up again, and with a little effort pulled itself inside the shaft and disappeared.

"Fuck," Spud said, stepping back and eyeing the ceiling.

"How do we stop it?" Grey asked.

"We need to shut down the air system," Glossy said, "try to block it in this part of the ship."

"Let's get to the flight deck now!" Nikita said.

"Go!" Grey said, pushing her down the corridor. "Everyone stick together!"

They moved swiftly down the corridor toward the flight deck. Upon reaching it, Nikita burst through the door and threw herself in her chair, hands darting here and there, closing the air vents and firing up the comms.

"What channel?"

"JV34," Grey said, sliding into the chair beside her, as the rest squeezed into the small flight deck space, or hugged the doorway into the corridor.

Nikita did her thing and gave Grey a nod.

"*Saputra*, this is Lieutenant Eve Grey. Requesting back up. We have four dead. I repeat we have four dead."

They watched Grey intently, one or other of them glancing up at the ceiling every now and then for any sign of the Panthera-X03 above them.

"I know," Grey said. "Tell the colonel we need backup. Now!"

Spud reached forward and opened a compartment beside Grey, pulling out two small laser-fire pistols. He handed one to Nikita, who took it and tucked it into her belt.

"Mine's in my cabin," Finn said.

Spud nodded. "We'll get it."

"Then put me through to the colonel," Grey said firmly. "That's an order... Did you hear me?"

They watched as Grey listened to whoever spoke on the other end, her brow furrowing further with every second that passed.

"Colonel, I—" She stopped. "Yes, sir... Sir, there's only two of us left... I understand but—" Grey listened intently for a moment, then hung her head slightly, closing her eyes. "...Yes, sir." She reluctantly ended the comms.

"What'd they say?" Spud asked her, sensing something was wrong.

She looked at him. "This ship has security cameras?"

Spud nodded. "Yeah. Why?"

"They hacked in, saw the whole thing."

"So they're sending in backup right?" Spud asked.

Grey shook her head. "No."

"No?" Nikita asked, eyebrows jumping to the top of her forehead.

"They're not risking anyone else just yet," Grey said.

"They're only two of us left!" Shaw said.

Grey looked at Spud. "They know you're ex-navy." She looked around at all of them. "As of now, you're back on the job. We need to contain this thing. Then they'll rescue us."

"What?" King said, his face paling and his forehead visibly sweating.

"We're *ex*-navy, Grey," Spud said. "As in, haven't served, or *trained*, for some time. You'll have younger, fresher legs on that ship of yours."

"I only have a skeleton crew left on my ship. I can't send them in. The admiral is sending a larger vessel, but it won't be here for several hours. We're on our own until then."

"We're on our own?" King said, leaning back against the wall as though the wind had been knocked out of him.

"It doesn't matter," she said. "You know how to fire a weapon, don't you?"

"We're a cargo ship, our weapons are small," Finn said, motioning to Spud's pistol.

"Unless we go back to the cargo hold and use the ones Grey's team left behind," Spud said.

"Jesus." Miguel shook his head, performing the sign of the cross upon himself.

"Right now, we don't have a choice," Grey said. "That thing is loose on this ship and if we don't trap it or take it out it will kill more of us. Do you understand?"

"How much can it eat?" Miguel asked.

"It's not about eating," Finn said. "It's about eliminating threats. That's what a weapon like this is designed for. To kill everything in its path."

Spud ran his hand over his face, then looked at his team. "First thing we do is stock up on weapons. We've got these two pistols," he motioned to his and the one he handed to Nikita, "and Finn's got a couple more in the store."

"I have some big knives in the mess," Miguel said.

"What about Shayla's gun?" Nikita said, looking around for it.

"Wait," Spud said, looking around at the faces on the flight deck and peering out the doorway into the corridor. "Where is Shayla?"

An alarm suddenly sounded on the flight deck console.

Nikita's eyes flew wide. "It's the escape pod." She snapped her face to Spud. "It's preparing to launch!"

Spud's face tightened. "Oh, no she didn't..." He spun around and charged back into the corridor.

"Spud! Wait!" Nikita called.

"I'll go with him!" Finn yelled, following behind.

"Shaw! Go too!" Grey barked.

● ● ●

Spun ran down the corridor as fast as he could.

"I'm gonna kill her," he muttered to himself. "I'm going to *fucking* kill her."

He thundered along until he burst through the doorway to the escape pod dock. He raced to the ladder stair, slid down it with speed, hit the ground and ran for the pod doors.

"Shayla!" he yelled, banging on the doors. "Shayla, stop!"

She looked at him through the pod's observation window, then darted her eyes to the console panel, finishing her preparations.

"Dammit!" Spud slapped the window, then moved to the control panel on the wall.

"Can we override it?" Finn asked, coming to a panting stop beside him.

"I'm trying! Nik?" he yelled into the comms speaker. "Can you stop it?"

"I can't," she replied. "She's removed our access. You need to stop her!"

"Shit!" he yelled, then ran back to the window and smacked it desperately. "Shayla! Shayla, don't do this!"

"I'm sorry, Spud," she said over the pod's speakers, then gave a sad smile. "Thanks for the ride." She pulled a lever down, sending air blasting into the compartment.

"Spud!" Finn yelled, grabbing him. "We need to get out of here, now!"

"SHAYLA!" Spud yelled, and Finn pulled him back.

"*Now*, Spud!"

They moved back toward the stairs, and Spud began to feel a compression inside his skull as the pressure began changing on the dock. He stumbled once, Finn too, but they helped each other up.

"Hurry!" Shaw yelled from the top of the stairs, grabbing them and pulling them through the doorway. As soon as they were through, Shaw sealed the door.

Spud stumbled to his feet, shaking off his dizzy head, and moved to the comms panel by the door. He turned on the external camera and watched as Shayla departed the *Benobi* in the only escape shuttle they had.

"You... *bitch*!" he yelled after her, panting as he caught his breath.

"If you so much as *think* of hooking up with her again," Finn panted also, "I'm going to help Nikita beat the shit out of you."

Spud looked at him. "Oh, I'm done. *Never* again."

"So, we're stuck here now," Shaw nodded. "That's just great!"

Suddenly, a vibration shook the ship and a white light lit up the screen. They winced at the brightness, felt the ship rumble, then turned back to see the escape pod had been blown apart into a ball of debris.

"What the...?" Spud said, mouth agape. "What just happened..?"

"The *Saputra*," Shaw said in shock. "They blew it up."

"They what!" Spud said, eyes popping.

Finn looked at him, equally shocked.

Shaw nodded to himself in understanding. "They couldn't risk the Panthera being aboard."

"Or the knowledge of it getting out," Finn said, locking concerned eyes with Spud.

Spud looked at the screen, heard pieces of debris hitting the sides of the *Benobi* as they flew past.

Pieces of Shayla.

Then a *meow* sounded above them.

They stiffened and looked up at the ceiling. Shaw and Spud raised their weapons high.

"Where is it?" Shaw asked.

Spud held his finger to his mouth angrily, motioning for him to shut up.

They each held still; the only sound, their heavy breathing.

Then they heard banging in the distance…

And yelling.

Spud listened carefully. It was Miguel.

"Hey, pussy cat! You want some dinner! Come and get it!"

They heard the *meow* deepen to a growl, then heavy footsteps above them suddenly padded away in Miguel's direction.

"What the hell is he doing?" Finn hissed.

"Rescuing us," Spud said. "Let's go!"

CHAPTER TEN

Spud raced back down the corridor toward the flight deck.

"Go grab your weapons," he called over his shoulder to Finn. "Shaw, go with him."

"What about you?" Finn asked.

"I'm good," he said, holding up his pistol. "Go! We need more weapons!"

Finn gave a nod and turned left down the corridor, heading to his cabin. Shaw followed. Spud ran on ahead for a little, then slowed as he tried to hear where Miguel was at.

He heard banging coming from the mess and made his way quietly toward it.

As he approached the door, he slid along the wall, weapon ready at his chest.

He listened again and heard the deepened growl.

"Back away!" he heard Grey hiss quietly. "Get behind me."

Spud peered around the doorway, saw Grey and Miguel standing outside the chillroom, staring at the roof. The small mess was in disarray – the tables and chairs knocked over and pushed into the corner – the banging must've been Miguel throwing the sturdy furniture about. They darted their eyes to Spud peering around the doorway, then looked back to the roof. Grey motioned for Miguel to head for the door.

Miguel nodded and slowly began to move, two large knives shining in his hands. Spud stepped into the mess, eyeing the air vent above, just inside the door, nervously. He motioned them both forward hurriedly. If the Panthera made it past them to the vent, they'd be trapped in the mess. Grey eyed the vent too, then began to move toward the small kitchen beside the chillroom. Spud's eyes popped frantically at hers, questioning. She reached out and grabbed a bowl off the bench and threw it on the floor with a loud clang.

The deep growl sounded, travelling in her direction. Spud waved Miguel out the door and moved toward Grey, beckoning her forward. She hurried toward him and they headed for the threshold, but the Panthera's fast padding thundered overhead and it suddenly burst through the air vent.

Spud skidded and fell backward to the ground as the muscled creature landed on the floor between him and Miguel. The creature looked around at Spud the easier target on his back, but Miguel raised his knives and roared at the Panthera, drawing its attention.

"Miguel, move!" Grey yelled, taking aim, but the creature quickly lunged at the *Benobi*'s cook – the bigger threat. Miguel continued his fierce roar as it knocked him back into the wall, then to the ground, and the cook kept stabbing his knives at it. They saw the silver blades slice up and over the shoulders of the beast. It screeched in pain but snapped its jaw on Miguel and shook him hard.

"Miguel!" Spud yelled. "No!"

A burst of flame flew over Spud's head as Grey fired. The beast screeched again, then turned its bloodied, camouflaged snarl to them.

"Move! Move!" Spud yelled, jumping up to his feet and pushing her backward.

"Where?" she yelled back, stepping around him to throw more flame at the creature and hold it back. Spud spotted the garbage chute in the wall beside the chillroom.

"Garbage chute! Go!"

They ran toward the mess chute as the Panthera came in at them. Grey switched her weapon over from flame to laser and fired, but the Panthera deftly snaked out of the way - its movements so swift as it partially ran up the wall.

Spud opened the chute door. "Get in!"

"You first!"

They heard Miguel shout and saw him staggering his bloodied body up behind the Panthera, knives in the air.

"Miguel, no!" Spud called to him. "Run!"

The Panthera turned around.

"Get out... of my... *mess*!" Miguel breathed in pain to the creature, raising his knives.

"Miguel!" Spud yelled, then turned to Grey. "Go!" Spud grabbed her and pushed her into the open chute. She yelped as she fell down to the lower deck. He looked around at Miguel standing in the doorway only to see the Panthera lunge at him once more.

"MIGUEL!" he screamed.

The Panthera's jaw clamped around the cook's throat; it gave one hard shake of its head, and Spud heard Miguel's neck break from where he stood. The knives clattered to the floor and Spud watched in horror as Miguel's limp body hung from the creature's mouth. It gave one last vicious shake, dropped the body and looked around at Spud with those dark circles which sat beneath a veneer of pink skin, gulping down the flesh in its mouth.

Then it snarled and crouched down.

"Shit!" Spud said. He spun around and dived into the open chute, pulling the hatch shut behind him.

He fell several feet, landing in a large container of garbage. A loud bang sounded above, and he saw the Panthera smash through the hatch, pieces raining down on him. He scrambled to his feet and crawled out of the garbage to see Grey aiming her weapon.

"Move! Move!" he yelled, pushing her out the door of the refuse store, and slamming his hand on the lever to close the metal door behind them. They heard a thud inside as the Panthera landed on the garbage and another louder thud as it rammed against the door.

Spud and Grey jumped back startled, before they turned and started running again.

"Why the hell didn't you stay on the flight deck?" he asked her.

"Nikita put the heat sensors on. We saw it was almost on you, so we drew it away. Miguel wanted to get his knives."

"Yeah, and now Miguel's dead!"

"Saving your life!" she shouted back.

Spud reached the stairwell that would lead them back up to the flight deck level and paused. His face was screwed up in pain. "Goddamn it! We can't kill this thing on our own!"

"We're going to have to," she said, panting. "It can't seem to get through the metal doors. Is there any room without air vents?"

Spud trawled through his mind as they jogged up the stairwell to the upper deck. "The chillroom!" he said. "There're vents but they're too small for it to get through."

"Can you turn the cooling off?"

"Yeah. Or maybe we should turn it up like it was in the box?" Spud said reaching the top of the stairs, pistol out front. "Put the damn thing on ice."

"No, I mean for us. That's our last resort," Grey said. "We hide in there until someone comes to help us."

"I'd prefer to lock it in there and leave us out here."

"*Spud!*" He saw Finn and Shaw running toward them. Finn now carried a pistol and had several smaller weapons tucked in his belt.

"Miguel's dead!" Finn said, panting with dread as he reached them. "It got him."

Spud nodded, the words stinging him like deep infected cuts. "I know," he squeezed Finn's shoulder.

The Panthera suddenly burst from the mess doorway further down the corridor.

"Shit!" Spud yelled as Finn and Shaw spun around to see it.

"It climbed the chute!" Grey said in awe.

Shaw raised his weapon and fired. They watched, amazed, as the creature turned into its mirage-like state and raced up the wall out of the line of fire, moving with a speed Spud had not seen before. If it had been pissed before, it was now furious. In seconds, it was alongside Shaw and leaped at him. Shaw fell back with the creature on him. Finn, next in line, fired his pistol, but missed, and the Panthera bounced up and knocked him down too.

Spud and Grey fired haphazardly at the mirage as it raced up the walls and across the roof, leaving claw imprints in the metal. In a flash, it had moved back down the corridor and disappeared into the mess again.

"Jesus!" Grey puffed, as Spud raced toward Finn.

"Finn!" he pulled him up. "You alright?"

Finn coughed and they both looked down at the deep claw marks across his chest. "Oh, that hurts!" he groaned, as Grey raced past to Shaw.

"You're alright," Spud told Finn. "I got you."

"Shaw!" Grey yelled, shaking him. "Shaw!"

Spud saw the side of his neck was torn open. He heard footsteps and turned to see King and Glossy running their way.

"Come on," he called to Grey. "We gotta go!" He looked back to King and Glossy. "Grab Finn!"

He left Finn, scooting over to Grey and Shaw, keeping his eyes on the mess door. He just made out the miraged-X peering around the corner of the door at them. He snatched up Shaw's weapon, throwing the strap around his neck and grabbed at Grey's shirt. "Come on!" he yelled in her face, pulling her up.

She stumbled to her feet as the Panthera appeared again. Spud pulled up the larger weapon and fired a blast of flame at it. The creature hissed and pulled back.

He glanced over his shoulder and saw King and Glossy had Finn and were running up ahead. He turned back to the Panthera and blasted another heat wave, as Grey moved along beside him and did the same.

Together they moved backward, firing flame at the creature to hold it back.

Sensing no way past the heat in the corridor, it growled angrily, then retreated once more into the mess.

Sensing a respite, Spud and Grey turned without hesitation and raced toward the flight deck, crowding in behind the others and slamming the door shut behind them.

"Shut the flight deck vents!" Spud shouted.

"Already done!" Nikita called back, as Spud and Grey fell to their knees, panting and exhausted.

They took a moment to catch their breath, watching as King fussed over Finn's slashed chest. Finn groaned in pain.

"Is he going to be alright?" Spud asked, getting to his feet.

"I can stem the bleeding, but he'll probably need surgery," King said. "And I don't know what the bacteria, or whatever it is, will do to him."

A banging sounded on the ceiling.

"It's trying to get in," Nikita said, eyes on the ceiling. She turned to the controls and flicked a series of switches. There was a rushing sound of vented air and the Panthera gave a whine.

"Stay back, bitch!" Nikita hissed at the roof.

"We can't stay here," Glossy said. "There's only so much of our air we can purge."

Spud looked at Grey, still on her knees, who was staring down at the floor.

"Hey," he said, grabbing her shirt, trying to pull her upward. "Grey? Grey, look at me!"

She turned her eyes up to him. They were vacant with devastation. "I lost my whole crew..." she said, barely a whisper, as her eyes shone with remorse.

Spud clenched his jaw and nodded. "And I just lost one of mine. But we're gonna make it through this. Alright? We have to!"

She shook her head, glanced around the flight deck, then got to her feet. She looked back at Spud. "You need to get your crew to the chillroom. I'll create a diversion so you can get them there. Lock yourselves inside with food and water. I'll kill it. When I do, you come out and make an SOS."

"You can't kill it on your own," Spud said. "We've been trying and failing."

"I can with this," she said, pointing down to a device on her belt. "It's a controlled explosive."

"That's not a good idea on a ship with us on it," Glossy said.

"I could draw it down to the empty escape pod dock. Lock myself inside and do it."

"You're talking about killing yourself," Spud said.

"I'm talking about saving you," she countered.

"No," Spud said.

"It's my job."

"Well, this is my ship and I'm in charge here. You have no crew and right now the navy has deserted you. You have no authority anymore. I *do*, and I say no."

"Glossy has an idea," Nikita said. "I think you should hear it."

They looked at the *Benobi's* engineer.

"Wait!" Nikita barked, then flicked a series of switches. "Just turning off our cameras." She looked at Glossy and gave a nod.

"If you help us hack into the *Saputra's* systems," Glossy said to Grey, "we could remote-pilot your transport ship back to us."

Grey stared at her. "We'd still need to get past the Panthera."

"Do it," Spud said to Glossy and Nikita, then looked back to Grey. "If we can't kill that thing, then we need to get off the ship and blow it."

"You're gonna blow the *Benobi*?" Glossy asked Spud.

"I don't want to, but... I can get another ship, Glossy. I can't get another you." He smiled sadly. Glossy returned the smile and punched his arm. Spud's eyes drifted to Nikita's. He saw them shine back at his as she smiled and gave him a nod.

Grey exhaled heavily and leaned back against the wall. She patted her pocket and pulled out a stick of gum. She unwrapped it and put it in her mouth, then paused. She suddenly patted her other chest pocket and pulled out the syringe and vial of King's that she'd confiscated earlier. Spud stared at it.

"Can we use that for Finn?" Spud asked King. "Will it ease his pain?"

"No," King said.

"But—"

"It's not used for that, Spud." He averted his gaze to the floor.

"What's it for then?"

King hesitated, then looked up at him. "It's a poison."

"Poison?" Spud furrowed his brow.

King stared back at him. "It's not for getting high, Spud... It's for ending things."

Everyone stared at the medic.

King gave a sad smile. "But you always stopped me from using it... and I always thought maybe I'd just try living one more day."

"Oh, man..." Spud reached out and squeezed his shoulder.

King looked at him. "If I'd known this was the day I'd be living, I would've told you to go fuck yourself."

Spud gave a laugh, but his face soon melted back to sadness. "I'm so sorry I brought this on everyone."

The silence sat heavily around them.

"You didn't know," Nikita said quietly. "She played you."

"We opened the box," Grey said. "This isn't all your fault."

"Well, Shayla got hers," Nikita said coldly.

"Nik," Spud said quietly.

"Stop being so goddamn nice!" she snapped.

Finn groaned. "I hate to interrupt but I'm not feeling too good." He suddenly vomited all over himself.

"Shit!" Spud said, as they all jumped back from the splatter.

King moved to support Finn's head. Finn's face was pale and sweating and he was starting to drift in and out of consciousness. "He needs proper medical attention and isolation."

"We can't leave him alone. Not in that state," Glossy said.

"Glossy, Nikita," Spud said, "bring us the *Saputra's* transfer ship." He looked back at Grey and plucked the vial from her hands. He studied it then looked back at King. "Would this be enough to kill the Panthera you think?"

King shrugged. "It's enough to kill a horse. I know that much."

Grey looked at Spud. "We'd have to get close to it, to stab that in."

Spud nodded. "Yeah, we would."

CHAPTER ELEVEN

The creature growled and Nikita flushed the vents again.

"We're running low on O² in here," she said.

"How much longer?" Spud asked Glossy. He wasn't sure how long he could stay in the confined space with the smell of Finn's vomit and blood clouding what little air they had. Not to mention the dried blood all over Grey.

"I'm almost there," Glossy said, eyes fixed on one of the *Benobi's* flight desk monitors.

Spud looked at Grey. "Get ready to input your access codes."

Grey looked up from studying plans of the *Benobi's* layout, nodded, and moved closer to Glossy.

"Alright, hurry!" Glossy called. "Before they know we're in."

Grey slipped in front of the console and began tapping away. Spud held his breath, waiting.

"Okay... we're in the *Saputra's* security systems!"

"Now take their authority away," Glossy said. "Change it so that you have sole access."

Grey tapped away as Glossy and Nikita pointed to parts of the screen and talked her through it.

"Done!" Nikita said. "Ship is launching."

They sat silently for a moment, waiting, watching.

Grey suddenly looked up and pressed her fingers to her ear.

"Yes, sir?"

They watched as she stared coldly out of the *Benobi's* flight deck windows into the space beyond.

"I will stop the creature, sir," she said, "you have my word. But I will not allow these civilians to die. They will leave on the *Saputra's* transport, and I will stay behind and take care of the creature. If I fail, then you can blow the whole ship, but these people are innocent and they saved my life. You will not harm them... *No*, sir! You listen to me! I have on board Senator Whitlam's son, Spelton. The senator, who is a strong military ally. Spelton, whose brother is the highly decorated Timothy 'Tiberius' Whitlam. I don't think they will appreciate you murdering him in cold blood, do you? No... That's correct... So, the transport will be allowed to leave this vessel and you will allow it to dock on the *Saputra*... Thank you, sir." She ended the comms and looked at them.

"Spelton?" Glossy grinned at Spud. "Spelton's your real name?"

"I prefer Spud," he said, then looked back at Grey. "Are you going to leave me any secrets today, Grey?"

She smirked in response. "You all make for the transport," she said, getting back to business. "If you fail, try the chillroom, lock yourself inside and wait for rescue."

"And what are you going to do?" Spud asked.

"I'm going to draw it away."

"Then, I'm going with you."

"No," she said firmly.

"You can't do this alone, you need someone to watch your back."

"*You* need to go with these people. You're their ticket off this ship."

Spud shook his head. "*We* lure the creature away, while *they* get to the ship. If we can't kill it, then we wait for another unit to rescue us. I'm *your* ticket off this ship."

"Not if you're dead."

"We can try surviving, or we can die trying," Spud said. "Either way, I brought Shayla and that box onto my ship, and it's my responsibility that no more of my crew die trying to get off."

"You're a civilian," she shot back. "You said it yourself, you're a lover not a fighter."

"Yeah," he straightened, "well, today I'm fighting!"

"Look, Compton, it's honorable but—"

"Grey, I grew up playing war games with my brother while my father watched on the sidelines critiquing us. You think I didn't learn a thing or two play-fighting my brother? The *great* Tiberius Whitlam? You think the senator didn't teach me a thing or two about strategy?"

She stared at him as the team watched on.

"You want to do this to avenge your dead team," Spud said, "I get that. So, understand that I want to do this to keep mine alive."

"Do we get a say in this?" King asked.

"No. You don't," Spud said.

An alert sounded from the comms panel.

"Oxygen has hit critical levels," Nikita said. "We gotta get out of this room or reopen the vents."

Grey stared at Spud, then gave him a nod. "Alright. *We* lure it away." She plucked the vial back off Spud. "The rest of you get to the transport bay. Let's go."

Spud peered out the crack in the door. The corridor looked empty. He looked back at the team, now armed with the small cache Finn had collected earlier, and gave the signal for them to move forward. King and Glossy helped a semi-conscious Finn along, while Nikita and Grey took up the rear.

They crept silently into the corridor. Not that Spud thought it would make much difference. He tried to recall the pet cat his mom had had when he was a kid. Tried to think about its senses. He remembered the ears always twitching at noises he couldn't hear. Its nose smelling things, he couldn't smell. Its eyes glowing in the dark, seeing things he couldn't.

Now he just had to add 200–250 pounds of muscle to that, and infected claws, and the ability to camouflage…

Man, they were fucked.

He gripped Shaw's weapon tighter and checked how much oil he had left to flame. Not much. He had more in laser fire and stunner charge, but the flame was bigger and broader and would put much more of a gap between him and the creature.

He came to the first corner in the corridor, the one that led back to the cargo hold where the *Saputra's* shuttle would dock. He peered around the corner. It looked clear. He hurried across to the other side of the corridor, then motioned the others to move down it to the cargo hold. King, Finn and Glossy stared at him. Glossy's eyes shone and King's face looked saddened, while Finn was barely conscious at all, his face dripping with sweat, his pale skin now looking a shade of green. Spud hiked his thumb for them to leave. Nikita moved alongside them, ready to take the lead. She locked fierce eyes with Spud, the kind that told him he'd better follow them soon or she'd come back and kick his ass. He gave her a nod then turned to Grey.

"ALRIGHT!" he yelled. "LET'S GET THIS PARTY STARTED!" He smacked his fist on the walls, as his crew slunk away down the corridor.

"Party?" Grey said.

"Well, it's a hunting party, right?"

"Yeah, but who's doing the hunting?"

They heard the growl above them.

"Not us!" Spud said grabbing her and running.

They ran down the corridor, past the mess where Miguel's body lay, yelling and thumping the walls. The Panthera growled louder.

"It doesn't like the noise," Grey said.

"No," Spud agreed. "Shame about that! WOOOOOOO-HOOOOOOOO!" he yelled, banging and thumping more as they ran along. They heard a thump and a clatter behind them and spun around to see an air vent grille on the floor and the camouflaged Panthera landing on the ground. They paused, mesmerized by it. Spud admired its clear, mirrored surface, wondering how the hell the navy had managed to achieve that.

"She's kind of beautiful, isn't she?" he said in awe.

"What makes you think it's a she?"

Spud shrugged. "It has to be a woman. It's trying to kill me."

Grey scoffed. "Maybe you're just choosing the wrong women, Spud?" They exchanged a quick glance but turned back as the Panthera growled again and readied to pounce.

"RUN!" Spud yelled, as it launched. He lifted his weapon and sprayed a burst of flame.

"COME ON!" Grey yelled running off down the corridor. She paused after a while and took a turn to throw flame at the creature, while Spud ran past her. They continued to take turns running and throwing flame as the creature chased them.

"Goddamn, it's fast," Spud puffed, aiming up the walls as it tried every which way to reach them. "We're going to run out of corridor soon."

Grey pressed her finger to her ear. "The transport's docked!"

The Panthera paused listening to something in the distance.

"Oh, no you don't!" Spud yelled at it. "HEY! Look at me! Fresh meat right here!"

"Spud!" Grey yelled, pulling him back as the creature lunged again.

"Shit!" He shot flame at the creature, as it flew past him up along the wall.

The animal whined and skidded, rolling out its flames. The camouflage disappeared and it looked back at him, baring its bloodied teeth, its pink body black in parts from the burns it had received.

"Fuck," Grey panted. "We're supposed to be leading it away, but it's gotten past us."

The creature snarled and readied to pounce again.

"We just need to hold it a little longer and give the team a chance to load onto the transport chute," Spud asked.

"The chillroom!" Grey yelled. "Get to the mess now!"

The creature leaped at them again as they raced away. Spud tried throwing more flame, but it flickered, before dying. He was out of oil.

"Shit!" he said, switching it to laser, while Grey threw flame at the Panthera.

He saw the mess hall door up ahead, and Miguel's lifeless body lying in the corridor outside. Spud raced toward it and skidded through the door, as Grey paused in the doorway throwing more flame.

"I'm almost out!" she called to him.

"Just stall it while I get this open!"

Spud raced to the chillroom door, unlocked it and yanked it open.

The creature growled low and rumbling.

"It's sizing me up!" Grey called.

"Got it! Hurry!"

Grey's weapon coughed its last flicker, before she darted inside the mess. The creature hit the doorway soon after on her trail. Grey turned to face its attack as the creature lunged and knocked Grey down. Spud raced forward, went to spit laser at it, but the creature was too close and already on top of Grey, snapping at the weapon she held over her throat. Panicked, Spud barreled into the creature, knocking it off her.

"Spud!" she gasped, as he fell on top of the creature, they rolled, and skidded along the mess floor.

As they came to a stop, Spud found himself on top of the creature and thrust his gun across the creature's throat, trying to hold it down, but its claws dug in and sliced down his back.

Spud yelled in pain, then he was suddenly yanked aside, as a wall of heat flew past his face. The Panthera whined in pain, its skin smoking as it scuttled into the corner, scattering chairs. Spud looked up to see Grey dragging him away, and King standing in the doorway with what must've been one of the abandoned weapons from the cargo hold.

"King?" he said, confused.

"You saved me enough, Spud," King said, entering the room, grabbing him along with Grey and pulling him toward the chillroom. "It's time I saved you!"

King and Grey threw him into the chillroom and he slid along the floor, banging into the shelves. When he came to a stop, he looked back and saw them outside the door. King grabbed the syringe and vial from Grey's pocket, as the creature whined in the background.

"What are you doing?" she yelled at King.

"Shit!" King suddenly jumped aside and Grey darted inside the chillroom, behind the door, as the Panthera slammed into it.

Spud forced himself up with a struggle, the claw marks down his back hurting badly, and pressed his weight against the door, along with Grey, as the Panthera slammed into it, trying to get in.

The now dented door bounced open but another wall of flame burst past the doorway, as King fired from outside. The Panthera pulled back shrieking.

Spud pulled the door open and saw the Panthera— smoke wafting off its burned skin, vengeance clear in its eyes—stalking King, who backed away to the mess door, one hand on his weapon and one holding the syringe up to the vial in his mouth as he withdrew the fluid. As soon as the syringe was filled, he spat the vial away.

"Spud!" King called, sliding the readied syringe across the floor toward him. Spud scuttled painfully out the chiller door and grabbed it.

"Stab it in!" King yelled as the creature growled and lunged for him.

Grey swooped past, snatched the syringe from Spud's hands and ran at the creature while King blasted flame at it.

"Grey!" Spud yelled.

She leaped onto its back and stabbed the syringe hard into its neck. The creature shrieked again, mainly at the flame, as it reared and spun around, throwing Grey off into the wall, her arms singed from the heat. King threw more flame at it. The Panthera growled and swung back around to King, fiercely angry now, pink saliva flying out of its mouth. He fired again, but the flame spluttered and died.

"Ah, shit..." King said, glancing between his weapon and the creature.

"King!" Spud yelled, as the Panthera connected with his medic and they both flew through the doorway into the corridor. Spud raced toward them, and Grey pulled herself up off the floor.

"The fluid!" she rasped, winded. "I never plunged the fluid!"

King screamed in pain as the Panthera sunk its teeth in his shoulder, shaking him like a doll. Spud threw himself on top of the creature, grabbed the syringe still sticking out of the tough skin of its neck, and plunged the fluid in.

The Panthera shrieked and hissed and threw him off with such force he went skidding down the corridor, past Miguel's body, as the creature righted itself and lunged for him once again.

Spud saw a knife shining on the floor near Miguel and snatched it up. He threw it up defensively to stop the creature's mouth snapping at him. Its teeth clashed with the steel and it backed up a step, as Grey appeared over its head with her weapon. She slammed the butt down hard on its skull. It snapped around at her, half growling, half groaning, and she pulled her weapon up to fire on it. The Panthera scuttled off Spud and down the corridor a little as Grey took aim.

But then she paused.

Spud saw the Panthera walking funny, shaking its limbs like it was trying to shake off some dirt.

It banged into the wall and gave a tiny kitten *meow*.

Then it made a hocking noise in its throat. It looked up at them with skin-covered eyes that said it wanted to kill them both, but then the look faltered and it vomited on the floor.

"The poison," Spud breathed, pained. "It's working!"

"Not fast enough," Grey said, then took aim and fired her laser weapon. The creature's head flew back and it fell over, smoke wafting up from its skull. It lay still for a moment, then its legs shook, and it meowed.

"*Goddamn it*, why won't this thing die!" Grey hissed. She stormed over to it and fired again and again until it stopped moving, leaving a crisscross pattern of laser wounds over its body.

Then, finally, with a tiny *meow*, the creature stilled. Dead.

Panting with exertion, her arms singed, Grey looked back at Spud. They exchanged a look of relief, before he lay his head back on the floor.

But King's groan roused him again.

Spud urgently pulled himself up, wincing all the while, the claw wounds on his back burning now like molten flame. He rushed to King's side and pulled him up to lay in his arms. King's throat and chest were wounded badly.

"King..." he said softly, eyeing the damage, concerned. He pressed his hand over the wound.

"It's okay," King said faintly through bloodied teeth. "They made it to the transport. They're safe. Nikita wasn't leaving without you."

"But, you..."

King smiled faintly. "I couldn't live knowing you were going to die for me," he said, then coughed, splattering blood. Grey knelt down on the other side of him. King's eyes watered as he stared at Spud. "It's okay, Spud."

Spud clasped his hand over the medic's. "King..."

"I'm... okay... with dying..." he managed, before his face fell slack.

"King?" Spud said. "No! King!" He shook him.

Grey reached out and held Spud's arm to console him.

Spud squeezed his eyes shut for a moment in sorrow. He suddenly felt dizzy and opened his eyes again. He lowered King's body to the ground, as his back burned with an intense heat.

Suddenly the dizziness swam all over him and he turned and vomited heavily over the floor.

"Spud?" Grey looked at him concerned.

He saw two of her spinning in his vision. "My back..."

"Spud?" she said again faintly, before everything turned black.

CHAPTER TWELVE

Spud slowly arose to consciousness in a white-walled room. He heard beeping, looked over and realized it was a heart monitor. His heartbeat.

He was alive.

He looked down at the bed, saw he was dressed in a hospital gown. He moved to sit up and realized his right wrist was cuffed to the bed. The other was attached to a drip. He lay back down, feeling the stinging cuts on his back and groaned a little. He stared at the ceiling, wondering where he was. Wondering where his team was. He looked at the handcuff and wondered if it had been Grey.

He wasn't sure how long he'd laid there, but soon enough, the tiredness washed over him again, his eyes began to blink heavily, and he sunk into the dark depths of sleep once more.

Three times he awoke. Twice he'd fallen back unconscious. Upon waking the third time, a nurse hovered over him.

"Where am I?" he mumbled through the sleep. "Where's my team?"

The nurse didn't answer him, but then someone entered his room who he knew would.

Grey.

They locked eyes and he rubbed his face awake, as she walked slowly over to the bed. She nodded at the nurse, watched as she left, then turned back to Spud. Grey looked a little tired and bruised, her singed forearms lightly bandaged, but otherwise she was alright. Her blond curly hair was washed and pulled back in a bun.

"How're you feeling?" she asked softly, her green eyes studying him.

"Where's my crew?"

"They're fine. They've been seen to."

Spud stared at her.

"They're fine," she said firmly. "Finn, too. We're on the *Gabriel*."

"The admiral's ship?" Spud couldn't help but gape. "The admiral came and got us?"

"No, another ship came and brought us to him. You've been unconscious for a few days."

"I have?" He glanced around the room, confused. "I want to see them. My crew... And King and Miguel... their bodies, what did you—"

"Spud," she moved up beside him and placed her hand on his shoulder. "We have them. We have them all. It's going to be okay." She smiled softly, but then it faded. She stepped back again. "I think."

"You think?"

"The admiral wants to see us. As soon as you're up for it."

Spud sat up. "I'm good."

"Are you sure?" she asked eyeing him carefully as he swayed a little. "The Panthera's claws, they have this venom, a poison, it..."

"It what?"

"Your back, the cuts have almost healed. The venom, though, it put you in a coma, Spud. They gave you the anti-venom and it did its thing."

"Anti-venom?"

She nodded. "Exosis. They had the anti-venom you needed."

"And Finn got it too?"

"Yeah..."

"Well, let's go see them." He jangled the cuff.

She reached in her pocket for keys, then removed it. He rubbed his wrist, threw back the sheets and stood. She stepped back, flashing a smile.

"Are you sure you're okay?" she asked.

He nodded. "Yeah... Thanks to you. You did some crazy shit to help me."

She scoffed and smiled again. "Like you tackling the X off me?"

He smiled back. "Yeah... I've been known to do stupid things for women before."

She stared at him. "Well, this time you helped the right one."

They stood in silence for a moment, before she cleared her throat.

"Get dressed and meet us outside when you're ready."

He nodded and she moved for the door.

"Grey?"

She stopped and looked back. "Yeah?"

"One question," he said, eyes narrowed in study. "You're a very good soldier. I know what one looks like. So why were you stationed on a small ship patrolling The Wastelands?"

She looked at him, considering her answer. "A married colonel wanted me to be his plaything and I said no."

Spud's face softened. "So, they shipped you out there?"

She shrugged. "Well, I did break his arm."

"You broke his arm?" A smile slid across his face.

She nodded and a smile slid across her face too. "He wouldn't take no for an answer, so I had to make him understand my decision."

Spud's grin slowly faded. "I'm sorry to hear that."

She shrugged again. "It's alright. I know not all guys are like that."

"No," he said, "we're not."

She nodded and opened the door, then turned back to him.

"Oh, Spud, by the way... there's a mirror behind you. I can see your ass."

Spud turned around, saw the mirror, then quickly closed over the back opening of his hospital gown. He looked back to see her grinning as she walked out the door.

● ● ●

Spud, now dressed in a navy uniform—the only clothes available to him on this ship—was escorted by two guards into a large meeting room. When he arrived, he saw two men and Grey sitting at the table. One man he instantly recognized as the admiral: short, broad and dark-haired with a peppered mustache. Spud acknowledged him with a nod. The other man, maybe late-30s, and balding, he didn't know.

"Where's my crew?" he asked Grey.

"They're in their quarters," the unknown man answered.

"And you are?"

"I'm Lieutenant Carlton. Chief Science Officer."

"Your crew are fine," the admiral assured him.

"I'd like to see them, sir," he said, unable to stop himself falling back into military ways. It was a force of habit really. This *was* the admiral, after all.

"Take a seat, Compton," he said. "Or should I call you Whitlam?"

Spud darted a glance to Grey, as he pulled out a chair and took a seat. "I go by Compton, sir."

The admiral observed him carefully.

"Your father, Senator Whitlam, has been on transmission with me. He talked me around to treating you with leniency."

"Leniency?" Spud's eyebrows rose.

"You were caught with stolen goods. Navy goods."

"Goods I had no idea about, sir. Goods that killed two of my crew."

"So Lieutenant Grey tells me."

Spud cast her another look. She sat straight, eyes forward, in soldier mode.

"Well," the admiral said, "your father has negotiated a deal with the navy. One that will see you released."

"Really? I haven't seen or spoken to my father in some time, sir."

"That may be, but lucky for you, he still gives enough of a shit about you to step in and save your hide."

Spud glanced down into his lap, then looked up again. "You said he worked out a deal with you. That means you'll let me off for something in return?"

"It does."

"What do you want from me, sir?"

"You will rejoin the navy and undertake a special mission for us. If you succeed, we'll let you go, uncharged."

"Rejoin the navy?" Spud glanced at Grey again, then smiled. "I told my father a long time ago, I don't want to be a soldier. If he thinks this is a way to get me back in—"

"You'd rather sit in a jail? Would rather your crew sit in a jail?"

He glanced at Grey once more, then looked back at the admiral.

"I was medically discharged, sir," Spud said, tapping his thigh. "Bullet wound."

"Our doctors say you are mission fit and ready to go. They say there must've been an error with your prior medical record." The admiral's eyes narrowed at him. "Know anything about that?"

Spud stared back a moment. "No, sir. I do not."

He knew it was a long shot. It had only been a flesh wound after all. He sighed.

"So I do this mission and you let me *and* my crew go?"

"Yes."

"Alright, what's the mission?"

The admiral looked at Lieutenant Carlton. He gave the admiral a nod and began tapping away at a console embedded into the table. Soon, a 5D image appeared in the air of a green-blue planet.

"This," the man said, "is Bracken-Loti. It's a planet rich with minerals, ripe for mining. We've sent several teams down there to prepare habitats, ready for the mining companies to get to work. However, there was a problem with large rodents. Carnivores that attacked in packs. Everyone we sent down there, we lost contact with. So we prepared a defense to clear the rodents out. It worked. Too well. Now we have a problem with clearing the defense."

"Which was?" Spud asked.

Grey looked at him for the first time, with troubled eyes. A shiver ran down Spud's spine. He looked back at the admiral.

"Please tell me you didn't?" Spud said.

"Five Panthera-X03's were sent down there to sort the problem out. Now we need to remove them."

Spud stared at him speechless for a moment.

"Five…" Spud eventually said. "You have *five* more of those things?"

"And they need to be removed," the admiral said in all seriousness.

Spud burst into laughter and shook his head. "You'd better nuke the planet then."

"We can't. We won't risk it."

"The planet's core is," Carlton began, "er, temperamental. It's highly volcanic. Any form of explosive that could set off a chain reaction and destabilize things has been ruled out."

"Then poison," Spud said. "If you're going to mine the planet, you're not exactly giving a shit about the wildlife or natural habitat down there, are you?"

"We need humans to be able to work down there. Releasing poisons into the atmosphere won't do. Some of the vegetation down there is edible. We need to preserve what we can, while mining the resources."

"Wait, why are you telling *me* this?"

"Because," the admiral said, "you're going to go down there with a unit of soldiers, and capture the Panthera's for us."

Spud stared at him for a moment then began shaking his head. "Oh, no, no, no…"

"That's the deal arranged with your father," the admiral said.

Spud stared at him. "And you said my father gave a shit about me."

"He does," the admiral said, "because he's sending your brother in with you."

Spud paused, darting his eyes between the faces in front of him. "Tiberius? My father is sending in Tiberius' unit?"

"Yes," Carlton said. "You, your crew, Tiberius' unit... and Lieutenant Grey."

Spud looked at her. She stared back.

"I disobeyed orders," she said. "This is my ticket out too."

"If you're sending in Tiberius, then you don't need us," Spud said to the admiral.

"You have fought and overcome an X03," Carlton said. "That makes you an expert on the creature."

"That's the deal," the admiral said, standing up and buttoning his jacket. "Take it or leave it. *Compton*."

The admiral and Lieutenant Carlton swiftly left the room.

Spud stared at the image of the planet, Bracken-Loti, before him, a green-blue hologram floating midair above the conference table, bathing him in its green-blue hue. He looked at Grey.

"Are they serious?"

She nodded.

"I'm not a soldier anymore. Nor is my crew. We barely got off my ship with our lives facing only *one* of those things."

"I know," she said. "And now we have to face five of them... This is our punishment, Spud. But if we play our cards right, it can be our way out too."

Spud slowly leaned back against his seat and stared up at the ceiling.

"Shiiiiiit."

Join Spud's next action-packed adventure:

The Deepest Jungle (Spud Compton 2)
The Deftest Deceit (Spud Compton 3)

If you enjoyed reading *The Darkest Cargo* (Spud Compton 1), let people know! Leave a simple rating or write a brief review wherever you can. It means a lot to me, the author, and really helps with making this book visible to others.

To keep up to date with new releases visit:
amandabridgeman.com.au

Amanda Bridgeman